COMRADES

NORMAN CLASPED HER IN HIS ARMS.

COMRADES

A STORY OF SOCIAL ADVENTURE IN CALIFORNIA

BY

THOMAS DIXON, Jr.

Illustrated by
C. D. WILLIAMS

Fredonia Books
Amsterdam, The Netherlands

Comrades:
A Story of Social Adventure in California

by
Thomas Dixon, Jr.

ISBN: 1-4101-0804-X

Copyright © 2005 by Fredonia Books

Fredonia Books
Amsterdam, The Netherlands
http://www.fredoniabooks.com

DEDICATED TO
THE DEAREST LITTLE
GIRL IN THE WORLD, MY DAUGHTER
LOUISE

CONTENTS

LEADING CHARACTERS OF THE STORY

Scene: California. *Time:* 1898–1901

NORMAN WORTH	.	An Amateur Socialist
COLONEL WORTH	. . .	His Father
ELENA STOCKTON	.	The Colonel's Ward
HERMAN WOLF	. .	A Socialist Leader
CATHERINE . .	. .	His Affinity Wife
BARBARA BOZENTA	.	A New Joan of Arc
METHODIST JOHN	. . .	A Pauper
TOM MOONEY	. . . .	A Miner
JOHN DIGGS	. . .	A Truth Seeker
ROLAND ADAIR	. . .	Bard of Ramcat

COMRADES

COMRADES

CHAPTER I

THE WOMAN IN RED

FOOLS and fanatics!"

Colonel Worth crumpled the morning paper with a gesture of rage and walked to the window.

Elena followed softly and laid her hand on his arm.

"What is it, Guardie? I thought you were supremely happy this morning over the news that Dewey has smashed the Spanish fleet?"

"And so I am, little girl," was the gentle reply, "or was until my eye fell on this call of the Socialists for a meeting to-night to denounce the war — denounce the men who are dying for the flag. Read their summons."

He opened the crumpled sheet and pointed to its head lines:

"Down with the Stars and Stripes — up with the Red Flag of Revolution — the symbol of universal human brotherhood! Come and bring your friends. A big surprise for all!" The Colonel's jaws snapped suddenly.

"I'd like to give them the surprise they need to-night."

"What?" Elena asked.

"A serenade."

"A serenade?"

"Yes, with Mauser rifles and Gatling guns. I'd mow them down as I would a herd of wild beasts loose in the streets of San Francisco."

"Merely for a difference of opinion, Governor?" lazily broke in a voice from the depths of a heavy armchair.

"If you want to put it so, Norman, yes. Opinions, my boy, are the essence of life — they may lead to heaven or hell. Opinions make cowards or heroes, patriots or traitors, criminals or saints."

"But you believe in free speech?" persisted the boy.

"Yes. And that's more than any Socialist can say. I don't deny their right to speak their message. What I can't understand is how the people who have been hounded from the tyrant-ridden countries of the old world and found shelter and protection beneath our flag should turn thus to curse the hand that shields them."

"But if they propose to give you a better flag, Governor?" drawled the lazy voice. "Why not consider?"

"Look, Elena! Did the sun ever shine on

anything more beautiful? See it fluttering from a thousand house-tops — the proud emblem of human freedom and human progress! Dewey has lifted it this morning on the foulest slave-pen of the Orient — the flag that has never met defeat. The one big faith in me is the belief that Almighty God inspired our fathers to build this Republic — the noblest dream yet conceived by the mind of man. Dewey has sunk a tyrant fleet and conquered an empire of slaves without the loss of a single man. The God of our fathers was with him. We have a message for the swarming millions of the East——"

"Pardon the interruption, Governor, but I must hold the mirror up to nature just a moment — your portrait sketched by the poet-laureate of the English-speaking world. He speaks of the American:

> "Enslaved, illogical, elate.
> He greets the embarrassed gods, nor fears
> To shake the iron hand of Fate
> Or match with Destiny for beers.

> "Lo! imperturbable he rules,
> Unkempt, disreputable, vast —
> And in the teeth of all the schools
> I— I shall save him at the last!"

The Colonel smiled.

"How do you like the picture?"

"Not bad for an Englishman, Norman. You know we licked England twice ——"

"And we kin do it again, b' gosh, can't we?" blustered the younger man with mock heroics.

"You can bet we can, my son!" continued the Colonel, quietly. "The roar of Dewey's guns are echoing round the world this morning. The lesson will not be lost. You will observe that even your English poet foresees at last our salvation.

"'And in the teeth of all the schools
I—I shall save him at the last!'"

"Even in spite of the Socialists?" queried the boy, with a grin.

"In spite of every foe — even those within our own household. War is the searchlight of history, the great revealer of national life, of hidden strength and unexpected weakness. I saw it in the Civil conflict — I've seen it in this little struggle ——"

"Then you do acknowledge it's not the greatest struggle in history — that's something to be thankful for in these days of patriotism," exclaimed Norman, rising and stretching himself before the open fire while he winked mischievously at Elena.

"It's big enough, my boy, to show us the truth

about our nation. Our old problems are no longer real. The Union our fathers dreamed has come at last. We are one people — one out of many — and we can whip Spain before breakfast ——"

"With one hand tied behind our back!" laughed the boy.

"Yes, and blindfolded. It will be easy. But the next serious job will be to bury a half million deluded fools in this country who call themselves Socialists."

The Colonel paused and a look of foreboding clouded his face as he gazed from the window of his house on Nob Hill over the city of San Francisco, which he loved with a devotion second only to his passionate enthusiasm for the Union.

Elena sat watching him in silent sympathy. He was the one perfect man of her life dreams, the biggest, strongest, tenderest soul she had ever known. Since the day she crept into his arms a lonely little orphan ten years old she had worshipped him as father, mother, guardian, lover, friend — all in one. She had accepted Norman's love and promised to be his wife more to please his father than from any overwhelming passion for the handsome, lazy young athlete. It had come about as a matter of course because Colonel Worth wished it.

The Colonel turned from the window, and his eyes rested on Elena's upturned face.

"It will be bloody work — but we 've got to do it ——"

Elena sprang to her feet with a start and a laugh.

"Do what, Guardie? I forgot what you were talking about."

"Then don't worry your pretty head about it, dear. It 's a job we men will look after in due time."

He stooped and kissed her forehead "By-by until to-night — I 'll drop down to the club and hear the latest from the front."

With the firm, swinging stride of a man who lives in the open the Colonel passed through the door of the library.

"Norman, I can't realize that you two are father and son — he looks more like your brother."

"At least my older brother ——"

"Yes, of course, but you would never take him for a man of forty-eight. I like the touch of gray in his hair. It means dignity, strength, experience. I 've always hated sap-headed youngsters."

"Say, Elena, for heaven's sake, who are you in love with anyhow — with me or the Governor?"

A smile flickered around the corners of the girl's eyes and mouth before she slowly answered:

"I sometimes think I really love you both,

Norman — but there are times when I have doubts about you."

"Thanks. I suppose I must be duly grateful for small favours, or else resign myself to call you 'Mother.'"

"Would such a fate be intolerable?"

Elena drew her magnificent figure to its full height and looked into the young athlete's face with laughing audacity.

"By George, Elena, if I'm honest with you, I'd have to say no. You are tall, stately, dignified, beautiful from the crown of your black hair to the tip of your dainty toe — the most stunning-looking woman I ever saw. I never think of you as a girl just out of school. You always remind me of a glorious royal figure in some old romance of the Middle Ages ——"

"Now I'm sure I love you, Norman — for the moment at least."

"Then promise to go with me on a lark to-night," he suddenly cried.

"A lark?"

Elena's gray-blue eyes danced beneath their black lashes.

"Yes, a real lark, daring, adventurous, dangerous, audacious."

"What is it — what is it? Tell me quick."

The girl seized Norman's arm with eager, childish glee.

"Let's go to that Socialist meeting and beard the lion in his den."

Elena drew back.

"No. Guardie will be furious!"

"Ah, who's afraid? Guardie be hanged!"

"Go by yourself."

"No, you've got to go with me."

"I won't do it. You just want to worry your father and then hide behind my skirts."

"You can see yourself that's the easiest way to manage it. If he has a fit, I can just say that your curiosity was excited and I had to go with you."

"But it's not excited."

"For the purposes of the lark I tell you that it is excited. There's too much patriotism in the air. It's giving me nervous prostration. I want something to brace me up. I think those fellows can give me some good points to tease the Governor with."

"Tease the Governor! You flatter yourself, Norman. He doesn't pay any more attention to your talk than he would to the bark of a six weeks' old puppy."

"That's what riles me. The Governor's so cocksure of himself. I don't know how to answer him, but I know he's wrong. The fury with which he hates the Socialists rouses my curiosity. I've always found that the good things in life are forbidden. All respectable people are positively forbidden to attend a Socialist — traitors'— meeting. For that reason let's go."

"No."

"Ah, come on. Don't be a chump. Be a sport!"

"I'd like the lark, but I won't hurt Guardie's feelings; so that's the end of it."

"Going to be a surprise, they say."

"What kind of a surprise?"

"Going to spring a big sensation."

Elena's eyes began to dance again.

"The woman called the Scarlet Nun is going to speak, and Herman Wolf, the famous 'blond beast' of Socialism, will preside. They are mates — affinities."

"Married?"

"God knows. A hundred weird stories about them circulate in the under-world."

"I won't go! Don't you say another word!" Elena snapped.

Norman was silent.

"Are you sure it would be perfectly safe, Norman?" the girl softly asked.

"Perfectly. I know every inch of that quarter of the city — went there a hundred times the year I was a reporter."

"I won't go!"

"It's the wickedest street in town. They say it's the worst block in America."

"I don't want to see it." Elena laughed.

"And the hall is a famous red-light dancing dive in the heart of Hell's Half Acre."

"Hush! Hush! I tell you I won't — *I won't* go! But — but if I *do* — you promise to hold my hand every minute, Norman?"

"And keep my arm around your waist, if you like."

Elena's cheeks flushed and her voice quivered with excitement as she paused in the doorway.

"I'll be ready in twenty minutes after dinner."

"Bully for my chum! I'll tell the Governor we've gone for a stroll."

As the shadows slowly fell over the city, Norman led Elena down the marble steps of his father's palatial home and paused for a moment on the edge of the hill on which were perched the seats of the mighty. Elena fumbled with a new glove.

"Are you ready to descend with me to the depths, my princess in disguise?" he gaily asked.

"Did you ever know me to flunk when I gave my word?"

"No, you 're a brick, Elena."

Norman seized her arm and strode down the steep hillside with sure, firm step, the girl accompanying his every movement with responsive joy.

"You 're awfully wicked to get me into a scrape of this kind, Norman," she cried, with bantering laughter. "You know I was dying to go slumming, and Guardie would n't let me. It 's awfully mean of you to take advantage of me like this."

He stopped suddenly and looked gravely into her flushed face.

"Let 's go back, then."

"No! I won't."

Norman broke into a laugh. "Then away with vain regrets! And remember the fate of Lot's wife."

Elena pressed his hand close to her side and whispered:

"You are with me. The big handsome captain of last year's football team. Very young and very vain and very foolish and very lazy — but I do think you 'd stand by me in a scrap, Norman. Would n't you?"

"Well, I rather think!" was the deep answer, half whispered, as they suddenly turned a corner and plunged into the red-light district. His strong hand gripped her wrist with unusual tenderness.

"So who's afraid?" she cried, looking up into his face just as a drunken blear-eyed woman staggered through an open door and lurched against her.

A low scream of terror came from Elena as she sprang back, and the woman's head struck the pavement with a dull whack. Norman bent over her and started to lift the heavy figure, when her fist suddenly shot into his face.

"Go ter hell — I can take care o' myself!"

"Evidently," he laughed.

Elena's hand suddenly gripped his.

"Let's go back, Norman."

"Nonsense — who's afraid?"

"I am. I don't mind saying it. This is more than I bargained for."

The woman scrambled to her feet and limped back into the doorway.

Elena shivered. "I did n't know such women lived on this earth."

"To say nothing of living but a stone's throw from your own door," he continued.

"Let's go back," she pleaded.

"No. A thing like this is merely one more reason why we should keep on. This only shows that the world we live in is n't quite perfect, as the Governor seems to think. These Socialists may be right after all. Now that we 've started let 's hear their side of it. Come on! Don't be a quitter!"

Norman seized her arm and hurried through the swiftly moving throng of the under-world — gambling touts, thieves, cut-throats, pick-pockets, opium fiends, drunkards, thugs, carousing miners, and sailors — but above all, everywhere, omnipresent, the abandoned woman — painted, bedizened, lurching through the streets, hanging in doorways, clinging to men on the sidewalks, beckoning from windows, singing vulgar songs on crude platforms among throngs of half-drunken men, whirling past doors and windows in dance-halls, their cracked voices shrill and rasping above the din of cheap music.

Elena stopped suddenly and clung heavily to Norman's arm.

"Please, Norman, let 's go back. I can't endure this."

"And you 're my chum that never flunked when she gave her word?" he asked with scorn. "We are only a few feet from the hall now."

"Where is it?"

"Right there in the middle of the block

where you see that sign with the blazing red torch."

"Come on, then," Elena said, with a shudder.

They walked quickly through the long, dimly lighted passage to the entrance of the hall. It was densely packed with a crowd of five hundred. Elena closed her eyes and allowed Norman to lead her through the mob that blocked the space inside the door. At the entrance to the centre aisle he encountered an usher who stared with bulging eyes at his towering figure. Norman leaned close and whispered:

"My boy, can you possibly get us two seats?"

"Can I git de captain er de football team two seats? Well, des watch me!"

The boy darted up the aisle, dived under the platform, drew out two folding-chairs, placed them in the aisle on the front row, darted back, and bowed with grave courtesy.

"Dis way, sir!"

Norman followed with Elena clinging timidly and blindly to his arm. In a moment they were seated. He offered the boy a dollar.

The youngster bowed again.

"De honour is all mine, sir. But you can give it to the Cause when they pass the box."

Norman turned to Elena. "Well, does n't that

jar you ?   A sixteen-year-old boy declines a tip, and says give it to the Cause!"

The boy darted up the steps of the platform and whispered to the chairman:

"Git on to his curves! Dat's de captain o' de football — de bloke dat's worth millions, an' don't give a doggone!"

A woman dressed in deep red who sat beside the chairman leaned close and asked with quiet intensity:

"You mean young Worth, the millionaire of Nob Hill ?"

"Bet yer life! Dat's him!"

The woman in red whispered to the chairman, who nodded, while his keen gray eyes flashed a ray of light from his heavy brows as he turned toward Norman.

The woman wheeled suddenly in her chair, and with her back to the audience bent over a girl who was evidently hiding behind her.

"Outdo yourself to-night, Barbara. Young Norman Worth, the son of our multi-millionaire nabob, is sitting in the aisle just in front of you. Win him for the Cause and I'll give you the half of our kingdom."

"How can I know him ?" the girl asked excitedly.

"He's not ten feet from the platform in the

centre aisle — front row — clean shaven — a young giant of twenty-three — the handsomest man in the house. Put your soul *and* your body in every word you utter, every breath you breathe — and *win* him!"

"I 'll try," was the low reply.

CHAPTER II

A NEW JOAN OF ARC

THE woman in scarlet rose, lifted her hand, and the crowd sprang to their feet to the music of the most stirring song of revolution ever written.

Norman and Elena were both swept from their seats in spite of themselves. Elena's eyes flashed with excitement.

"What on earth is that they are singing, Norman?" she whispered.

"The Marseillaise hymn."

"Isn't it thrilling?" she gasped.

"It makes your heart leap, does n't it?"

"And, heavens, how they sing it!" she exclaimed.

Norman turned and looked over the crowd of eager faces — every man and woman singing with the passionate enthusiasm of religious fanatics — an enthusiasm electric, contagious, overwhelming. In spite of himself he felt his heart beat with quickened sympathy.

He was amazed at the character of the audience. He had expected to see a throng of low-browed brutes. The first shock he received was the feeling that this crowd was distinctly an intellectual one. They might be fanatics. They certainly were not fools. The stamp of personality was clean cut on almost every face. They were fighters. They meant business and they did n't care who knew it. Some of them wore dirty clothes, but their faces were stamped with the power of free, rebellious thought — a power that always commands respect in spite of shabby clothes. He looked in vain for a single joyous face. Not a smile. Deep, dark eyes, shining with the light of purpose, mouths firm, headstrong, merciless, and bitter, but nowhere the glimmer of a ray of sunlight! He felt with a sense of awe the uncanny presence of Tragedy.

And to his amazement he noticed a lot of men he knew in the crowd — three or four authors, a newspaper reporter evidently off duty, two college professors, a clergyman, three artists, a priest, and a street preacher.

The hymn died away into a low sigh, like the sob of the wind after a storm. The crowd sank to their seats so quietly with the dying of the music that Norman and Elena were standing alone for an instant. They awoke from the spell, and dropped into their seats with evident embarrassment.

A boy of sixteen stepped briskly to the front in answer to a nod from the chairman, and recited a

Socialist poem. After the first stanza, which was crude and stilted, Norman's eye rested on the heavy figure of the chairman. He was surprised at the power of his rugged face. Through its brute strength flashed the keenest sense of alert intelligence — an intelligence which seemed to lurk behind the big, shaggy eyebrows as if about to spring on its victim. His heavy-set face was covered with a thick, reddish blond beard and his short hair stood up straight on his head, like the bristles of a wild boar. Of medium height and heavy build, with arms and legs of extraordinary muscle and big, coarse short fingers evidently gnarled and knotted, by the coarsest labor in youth, he looked like a blacksmith who had taken a college course by the light of his forge at night. There was something about the way he sat crouching low in his seat, watching with his keen gray eyes everything that passed, that bespoke the man of reserve power — the man who was quietly waiting his hour.

"By George, a pretty good pet name they've given him — 'The Blond Beast,'" Norman muttered. "I should n't like to tackle him in the dark."

The woman in red leaned toward the chairman and said something in low tones. He nodded his massive head, smiled, and looked back over his shoulder at the girl sitting behind them.

The movement showed for the first time a long ugly scar on the side of his great neck.

"Look at that fellow's neck!" whispered Elena.

"Yes. He had a close call that time," Norman answered. "But I 'll bet the other one never lived to tell the story ——"

"Sh! 'The Scarlet Nun' is going to speak."

The woman in red rose and walked to the edge of the platform. She stood silent for a moment, her tall, graceful, willowy figure erect and tense. The crowd burst into a tumult of applause. She smiled, bowed, and lifted her slender hand with a quick, imperious gesture for silence.

Norman was struck by the note of religious fervour which her whole personality seemed to radiate. The peculiar scarlet robe she wore accented this impression perhaps, and its strangeness added a touch of awe. The dress gave one the impression of a nun's garb except that its long folds were so arranged that they revealed rather than concealed the beautiful lines of her graceful figure. The colour was the deep, warm red of the Socialist flag — the colour of human blood, chosen as the symbol of the universal brotherhood of man. The effect of a nun's cowl was given by a thin scarlet mantilla thrown over the head, the silken meshes of its long fringe mingling with the waves of her thick black hair. Her face was that of a madonna of the slender type, except that the lips were too full, round, and sensuous and her long eyelashes drooped slightly over dark, lustrous eyes.

"Comrades," she began, in slow, measured tones, "after to-night I retire from the platform to take up work for which I am better fitted. I promised you a big surprise this evening, and you shall not be disappointed ——"

A murmur rippled the audience and she paused, smiling into Norman's face with a curious look. She spoke with a decided foreign accent with little moments of coquettish hesitation as though feeling for words. Norman felt an almost irresistible impulse to help her.

"I am going to in-tro-duce to you to-night," she continued, "a new leader, whose tongue the God of the poor and the outcast and the dis-in-heri-ted has touched with divine fire. She is no stran-ger. Twenty years ago she was born beneath the bright skies of Cal-i-for-nia at Anaheim, in the little Socialist colony of Polish dreamers led by Madame Modjeska, Count Bozenta, and Henry Sienkiewicz, the distin-guished author of 'Quo Vadis.' As you know, the colony failed. Her mother died in poverty and she was placed in an orphan asylum until eight years of age, when she was taken back to Poland by her foolish kins-men.

Four years later I found her, a ragged, homeless waif, in the streets of Warsaw, alone and star-ving. Since then she has been mine. Amid the squalor and misery of the old world her busy little tongue never tired telling of the glories of Cali-for-nia! Always she sighed for its groves of oranges and olives, its dazzling flowers, its luscious grapes, its rich valleys, its cloud-kissed, snow-clad mountains and the mur-mur of its mighty seas! It was her tiny hand that led me across the ocean to you. I have sent her to school in one of your Western colleges where a great Socialist professor has taught her history and e-con-omics. I have the high honour, comrades, of intro-ducing to you the child of genius who from to-night will be the Joan of Arc of our Cause, Comrade Barbara Bozenta!"

She quickly turned and drew forward a trembling slip of a girl whose big brown eyes were swimming in tears of excitement. A moment of intense silence, and the crowd burst into cheers as the dazzling beauty of their new champion slowly dawned on their understanding. The woman in red resumed her seat, and the girl stood bowing, trembling, and smiling.

The young athlete watched her keenly. Never had he seen such a bundle of quivering, pulsing, nervous, ravishing beauty. He could have sworn he saw electric sparks flash from the tips of every eyelash, from every strand of the mass of brown curls that circled her face and fell in rich profusion on her shoulders and across her heaving bosom. He felt before she had uttered a word — felt, rather than saw — the remarkable effectiveness of the simple, girlish dress which enhanced her dark beauty. She wore the same deep red as the older woman, but the bottom of the skirt was relieved by a row of ruffles edged with white lace. A scarf of white embroidered at the ends with scarlet flowers, was thrown gracefully around her shoulders and hung below the knees. Her round young arms were bare to the elbows, her throat and neck bare to the upper edge of the full bust.

The girl's eyes sought Norman's for an imperceptible instant and a smile flashed from her trembling lips. The cheering ceased and she began to speak. He watched her with breathless intensity, and listened with steadily increasing fascination. Her voice at first was low, yet every word fell clear and distinct. Never had he heard a voice so tender and full of expressive feeling — soft and mellow, sweet like the notes of a flute. There was something in its tone quality that compelled sympathy, that stole into the inner depths of the soul of the listener, and led reason a willing captive.

In simple yet burning words she told of the darkness and poverty, the crime and shame, hunger and cruelty of the old world in which she had spent four years of her childhood. And then in a flight of poetic eloquence, came the story of her dreams of California, the Golden West, the land of eternal sunshine and flowers. And then, in a voice quivering and choking with emotion, she drew the picture of what she found — of Hell's Half Acre, in which she stood, with its brazen vice, its crime, its hopeless misery, its want and despair. With bold and fierce invective she charged modern civilization with this infamy.

"Why do strong men go forth to war?" she cried, looking into the depths of Norman's soul. "Here is the enemy at your door, gripping the soft, white throats of your girls. Watch them sink into the mire at your feet and then down, down into the black sewers of the under-world never to rise again! I, too, call for volunteers. For heroes and heroines — not to fight another — I call you to a nobler warfare. I call you to the salvation of a world. Will you come? I offer you stones for bread, the sky for your canopy, the earth for your bed, and for your wages death! None may enter but the brave. Will you come —— ?"

The last words of her appeal rang through

Norman's heart with resistless power. Her round, soft arms seemed about his neck and his soul went out to her in passionate yearning. He gripped the chair to hold himself back from shouting:

"Yes! I'm coming!"

She sank to her seat before the crowd realized that she had stopped. A shout of triumph shook the building — wave after wave, rising and falling in ever-increasing intensity. At its height the Scarlet Nun sprang to her feet, with a graceful leap reached the edge of the platform, and again lifted her hand. A sudden hush fell on the crowd.

"Now, comrades, the battle-hymn of the Republic set to new music! Mark its words, and remember that we sing it not as a mem-ory, but as a proph-esy of the day our streets may run red with the blood of the last struggle of Man to break his chains of Slav-ery — a proph-esy, remember, not a mem-ory! Read it Barbara!"

The girl was by her side in an instant, and read from memory, her clear sweet voice tremulous with passion:

"Mine eyes have seen the glory of the coming of the Lord;
He is trampling out the vintage where the grapes of wrath are stored;
He has loosed the fateful lightning of his terrible swift sword:
His truth is marching on!

I have seen Him in the watch-fires of a hundred
    circling camps ;
They have builded Him an altar in the evening's
    dews and damps ;
I can read His righteous sentence by the dim and
    flaring lamps :
His day is marching on!

He has sounded forth the trumpet that shall never
    call retreat ;
He is sifting out the hearts of men before His judg-
    ment seat;
Oh! be swift, my soul, to answer them, be jubilant
    my feet!
Our God is marching on!"

The crowd burst again into triumphant song,
and Norman looked at their faces with increasing
amazement. The immense vitality of their faith,
the rush of its forward movement, the grandeur and
audacity of their programme struck him as a
revelation. They proposed no half-way measures.
They meant to uproot the foundations of modern
society and build a new world on its ruins. Their
leaders were fanatics — yes. But fanatics were
the only kind of people who would dare such things
and do them. Here was a movement, which at
least meant something — something big, heroic,
daring. His face suddenly flushed and his heart
leaped with an impulse.

"In heaven's name, Norman, what's the matter?" Elena asked.

The young poet-athlete looked at her in a dazed sort of way and stammered:

"Did you ever see anything like it?"

"No, and I don't want to again," she replied with a frown. "Let 's go home."

"Wait, they are taking up a collection. At least we must pay for our seats."

When the usher passed he emptied the contents of his pocket in the collection-box.

As the meeting broke up, the boy who placed their seats touched Norman on the arm.

"Let me introduce ye to her. I wants ter tell 'er ye er my friend — I 've yelled my head off for ye many a day on de football ground. Jest er minute. I 'll fetch 'er right down."

The boy darted up on the platform, and Norman turned to Elena:

"Shall we please the boy?"

"You mean yourself," she replied. "I decline the honour."

She turned away into the crowd as the boy returned leading Barbara.

Norman hastened to meet them at the foot of the platform steps.

"Dis is me friend, Worth, de captain of de football team, Miss Barbara," proudly exclaimed the boy.

Barbara extended her soft hand with a warm

friendly smile, and Norman clasped it while his heart throbbed.

"I congratulate you," he said, "on your wonderful triumph to-night."

"You were interested?" she asked, quietly.

"More than I can tell you," was the quick response.

"Then join our club and help me in my work among the poor," she urged, with frank eagerness. "We meet to-morrow afternoon at three o'clock. Won't you come?"

A long, deep look into her brown eyes — his face flushed and his heart leaped with sudden resolution.

"Thank you, I will," he slowly answered.

He joined Elena at the door and they walked home in brooding silence.

CHAPTER III

THE BIRTH OF A MAN

NORMAN stood silent and thoughtful before the fire in the dining-room, the morning after the meeting of the Socialists. His sleep had been feverish and a hundred half-formed dreams had haunted the moments in which he had lost consciousness with always the shining face of Barbara smiling and beckoning him on.

Elena silently entered and watched him a moment before he saw her.

"Still dreaming of the New Joan of Arc, Norman?" she asked with playful banter.

"I'm going to do it, Elena," he said, with slow, thoughtful emphasis.

"What? Marry her without even giving me the usual two weeks' notice?" Elena laughed.

"Now, is n't that like a woman! I was n't even thinking of the girl——"

"Of course not."

Norman laughed. "By Jove, you're jealous at last, Elena."

"You flatter yourself."

"Honestly, I was n't thinking of the girl——"

31

"Well, I 've been thinking of her. She haunts me. I like her and I hate her. I feel that she 's charming and vicious, of the spirit and flesh, and yet I can't help believing that she 's good. The woman who introduced her is a she-devil, and the man who presided over that meeting is a brute. It 's a pity she 's mixed up with them. What are you going to do — play the hero and rescue her from their clutches?"

"Nonsense. The girl is nothing to me, except as the symbol of a great idea. It stirs my blood. I 'm going to join the Socialist Club."

"Of which the fair Barbara is secretary."

"Come with me, and join too. We 'll go together to every meeting."

"Have you gone mad?" Elena asked, with deep seriousness.

"I 'm in dead earnest."

"And you think your father will stand for it?"

"That remains to be seen. I 'm going to tackle him as soon as he comes down to breakfast."

"Well, if I never see you again, good-bye, old pal." She extended her hand in mock gravity.

"I 'm not afraid of him."

"No, of course not!"

"You 're a coward, or you 'd stand by me. Wait, Elena, he 's coming now."

"Why stand by? You 're not afraid? I 'll

return in time for the inquest. Brace up! Remember Barbara. Be a hero!"

With a ripple of laughter she disappeared as the Colonel's footsteps were heard at the door.

Norman braced himself for the ordeal. He had never before dared to test his father's iron will. He had grown accustomed to see strong men bow and cringe before him, and felt a secret contempt for them all. They were bowing to his millions. And yet the boy knew with intuitive certainty that beneath the mask of quiet dignity and polished military bearing of the man he facetiously called "the Governor" there slumbered a will unique, powerful, and overbearing. More than once he had resented the silent pressure of his positive and aggressive personality. His own budding manhood had begun instinctively to bristle at its approach.

The Colonel started on seeing Norman, and looked at him with a quizzical expression.

"Was there an earthquake this morning, Norman?"

"I did n't feel it, sir — why?"

"You 're downstairs rather early."

Norman smiled. "I 've been a little lazy, I 'm afraid, Governor. But you know I was n't consulted as to whether I wished to be born. You assumed a fearful responsibility. You see the results."

The Colonel dropped his paper and looked at Norman a moment.

"Well, upon my word!" he exclaimed. "What 's happened?"

"The biggest thing that ever came into my life, Governor," was the low, serious answer.

"What?"

"The decision that hereafter I 'd rather be than seem to be, that I 'm going to do some thinking for myself."

"And what brought you to this decision?" the father quietly asked.

"I went last night to that Socialist meeting."

"Indeed!"

"Yes," he went on, impetuously, "and I heard the most wonderful appeal to which I ever listened — an appeal which stirred me to the deepest depths of my being. I think it 's the biggest movement of the century. I 'm going to study it. I 'm going to see what it means. What do you say to it?"

The boy lifted his tall figure with instinctive dignity, and his eyes met his father's in a straight, deep man's gaze.

The faintest smile played about the corners of the Colonel's mouth as he suddenly extended his hand.

"I congratulate you!"

"Congratulate me?" Norman stammered.

"Upon the attainment of your majority. Up to date you have written a few verses and played football. But this is the first evidence you have ever shown of conscious personality. You 're in the grub-worm stage as yet, but you 're on the move. You 're a human being. You have developed the germ of character. And that 's the only thing in this world that 's worth the candle, my boy. It 's funny to hear you say that the appeal of Socialism has worked this miracle. For character is the one thing the scheme of Socialism leaves out of account. A character is the one thing a machine-made society could never produce if given a million years in which to develop the experiment."

"And you don't object?" Norman asked with increasing amazement.

"Certainly not. Study Socialism to your heart's content. Go to the bottom of it. Don't slop over it. Don't accept sentimental mush for facts. Find out for yourself. Read, think, and learn to know your fellow man. When you 've picked up a few first principles, and know enough to talk intelligently, I 've something to say to you — something I 've learned for myself."

The boy looked at his father steadily and spoke with a slight tremor in his voice.

"Governor, you're a bigger man than I thought you were. I like you — even if you are my father."

"Thanks, my boy," the Colonel gravely replied, "I trust we may know each other still better in the future."

CHAPTER IV

AMONG THE SHADOWS

UNDER the tutelage of Barbara, the young millionaire plunged into the study of Socialism with the zeal of the fresh convert to a holy crusade.

At first he had listened to her stories of the sufferings of the poor and the unemployed with mild incredulity. She laid her warm little hand on his and said:

"Come and see. If you think that Socialism is a dream, I'll show you that capitalism is a nightmare."

He followed her down the ugly pavements of a squalid street into the poorest quarter of the city. She entered a dingy hall and pushed her way through a swarm of filthy children to the rear room. On a bed of rags lay the body of a suicide — a working-man who had shot himself the day before. The wife sat crouching on a broken chair, with eyes staring out of the window at the sunlit skies of a May morning in California. Her body seemed to have turned to stone and her eyes to have frozen in their sockets. Her hands lay limp in her lap, her shoulders drooped, her mouth hung hopelessly open. She was as dead to every sight and sound of earth as though shrouded and buried in six feet of clay instead of sunlight.

Barbara touched her shoulder, but she did not move.

"Have you been sitting there all night, Mrs. Nelson?" she asked, gently.

The woman turned her weak eyes toward the speaker and stared without reply.

"You have n't tasted the food I brought you," Barbara continued.

The drooping figure stirred with sudden energy, as if the realization of the question first asked had begun to stir her intelligence.

"Yes. I set up all night with Jim. He'd a-done as much fer me. There's nobody else that cared enough to come. Ye know it ain't respectful to leave your dead alone——"

"But you must eat something," Barbara urged.

"I can't eat — it chokes me." She paused a moment, and looked at Norman in a dazed sort of way. "I tried to eat and something choked me — what was it? O God, I remember now!" she cried, with strangling emotion. "They are going to bury him in the potter's field unless we can save him, and I know we can't. He's got an old mother way back East that thinks he's

doing well out here. Hit 'll kill her dead when
she finds out he wuz buried by the city."

"He shan't go to the potter's field," Norman
interrupted, looking out of the window

The woman rose, and tried to speak, but sank
sobbing:

"Thank God! Thank God! Thank God!"

When the first flood of grateful emotion had
spent itself, she looked up at Norman and said:

"You see, sir, he was n't strong, and kept losin'
his job in Chicago. We 'd heard about California all our lives. We sold out everything and
got enough to come. For two years we 've made
a hard fight, but it was no use. Jim could n't
git work. I tried and I could n't. Folks have
helped us, but he was proud. He would n't beg
and he would n't let me. He would n't sell his
gun. I think he always meant to use it that way
when he got to the end, and it come yesterday
when they give us notice to git out."

She staggered over to the bed and fell across
the body, sobbing:

"My poor old boy. He loved me. He was
always good to me. I tried to go with him. But
I could n't pull the trigger! I was afraid! I was
afraid!"

When they reached the street, Barbara lifted
her brown eyes to Norman's face and asked:

"What do you think of a social system that drives thousands of men to kill themselves like that?"

"To tell you the truth I never thought of it at all before."

"He would have been buried in a pauper's grave but for your help. I brought you here this morning because I knew you would save her that anguish when you understood."

"You knew I would?" he softly asked.

"I would n't have let you come with me if I had n't known it," she answered, earnestly.

"It's funny how many of us live in this world without knowing anything about it," he said, musingly.

"It would be funny were it not a tragedy," she answered, turning across the street to the next block. They paused at the entrance of another narrow hallway.

"My work as secretary of the club includes, as you see, a wide range of calls. I'm a dispenser of alms, the pastor of a great parish, the friend, adviser, and champion of a lost world, and you have no idea what a big world it is."

"I'm beginning to understand. What's the trouble here? Another suicide?"

"No — something worse, I think. A man who was afraid to die and took to drink. That's the way with most of them. None but the brave can look into the face of Death. This man is good to his family until he's drunk. Drink is the only thing that makes life worth the candle to him. But when he's under the influence of liquor he's a fiend. Last night he beat his wife into insensibility. This morning he sent one of the children for me."

They climbed two flights of rickety stairs and entered a room littered with broken furniture. Every chair was smashed, the table lay in splinters, pieces of crockery scattered everywhere, and the stove broken into fragments. Two bleareyed children with the look of hunted rabbits crouched in a corner. A man was bending over the bed, where the form of a woman lay still and white.

"For God's sake, brace up, Mary!" he was saying. "Ye must n't die! Ye must n't, I tell ye! Your white face will haunt me and drive me into hell a raving maniac. I did n't know what I was doin', old gal. I was crazy. I would n't 'a' hurt a hair of your head if I 'd 'a' knowed what I was doin'!"

He bowed his face in his coarse, bloated hands and sobbed.

The thin white hand of the wife stroked his hair feebly.

"It's all right, Sam. I know ye did n't mean it," she sighed.

Norman sent for a doctor, and left some money.

With each new glimpse of the under-world of pain and despair the conviction grew in Norman's mind that he had not lived, and the determination deepened that he would get acquainted with his fellow men and the place he called his home.

"You are not tired?" Barbara asked, as they hurried into the street.

"No, I 'm just beginning to live," he answered, soberly.

"Good. Then you shall be allowed the honour of accompanying me to the county jail, to the poorhouse, to the hospital, and to the morgue — the four greatest institutions of modern civilization. We must hurry. I 've another sadder visit after these."

As they hurried through the streets, Norman began to study with increasing intensity the phenomena presented in the development of Barbara's character. The more he saw of her, the more he realized the lofty ideals of her life, the more puerile and contemptible his own past seemed.

At the jail they found a boy who had been convicted of stealing and sentenced to the penitentiary. His old mother was ill. Barbara bore her last message of love.

They stopped at the poorhouse to see a curious old pauper who had become a regular attendant on the Socialists' meetings. He was called "Methodist John," because he was forever shouting "Glory, Hallelujah!" and interrupting the speakers. Barbara was the bearer of a painful message to John. Wolf had instructed her to keep him out of the meetings. She had decided to try a gentler way — to warn him against yelling "Glory" again under penalty of being deprived of a dish of soup of which he was particularly fond. The Socialist Club served this simple, wholesome meal to all who asked for it after its weekly meetings.

John promised Barbara faithfully to stop shouting.

"Remember, John," she warned him finally, "shout — no soup! No shout — soup!"

"I understand, Miss Barbara," he answered, solemnly.

"You see, sir," he said, apologetically, turning to Norman, "I get along all right till she begins ter speak, and when I hears her soft, sweet voice it seems ter run all down my back in little ticklin' waves clean down ter my toes, an' I holler 'Glory' before I can stop it!"

Norman laughed.

"I understand, old man."

"You feel that way yerself, don't ye, now, when she looks down into yer soul with them big, soft eyes o' hern, an' her voice comes a-stealin' inter yer heart like the music of the angels——"

Barbara's face lighted, and a slight blush suffused her cheeks as she caught the look of admiring assent in Norman's expression.

"That will do, John," she said, firmly. "Mr. Wolf was very angry with you yesterday."

"I'll remember, Miss Barbara," he repeated. "And God bless your dear heart fer comin' by ter tell me."

"I suppose he has no people living who are interested in him?" Norman asked, as they turned toward the Socialist hall.

"No. He came from a big mill town in the East. His children all died before they were grown, and he landed here with his wife ten years ago. When she died, he was sent to the poor-house. He hasn't much mind, but there's enough left to burst into flame at the memory of his children being slowly ground to death by the wheels of those mills. I've seen his dead soul start to life more than once as I've looked into his face from our platform. What an awful thing to see dead men walking about!"

"Yes. People who are dead and don't know it. I never thought of it before." Norman exclaimed.

They stopped in front of a house with a scarlet light in the hall, which threw its rays through a red-glass transom over a door of coloured leaded glass. The shadows of evening had begun to fall, and for the first time the girl showed a sign of hesitation and embarrassment.

"I hate to ask you to go in here with me, and I 'd hate worse to have you see me go alone. Yet I have to do it. My work leads me."

"I 'm going with you, whether you ask it or not," he firmly replied.

"Then words are useless," she said, simply, as she rang the bell.

A Negro maid opened the door, and smiled a look of recognition. "She ain't no better, miss. She 's been crying for you all day."

Barbara led the way up two flights of stairs to a small room in the rear, and entered without knocking. With a bound she was beside the bed on which lay a slender girl of nineteen. A mass of golden blond hair was piled in confusion on the pillow, and a pair of big, childish-looking blue eyes blinked at her through her tears.

"Oh! you 've come at last! I 'm so glad. It makes me strong to see you. Your face shines so, Barbara! They say I can't live, but it 's not so. I shall live! I 'm feeling better every day. It 's nonsense. The doctors have n't got any sense.

I wish you 'd get me one that knows something. Won't you, dear?"

"My friend, Mr. Worth, who has called with me, has kindly agreed to send you another doctor, little sister — that 's why I brought him to see you."

Norman extended his hand, and grasped the thin, cold one the girl extended. He felt the chill of death in its icy touch as he stammered:

"I 'll send him right away."

"Thank you," the girl replied, as a smile flitted about her weak mouth. She turned to Barbara with a look of infinite tenderness.

"I knew you 'd come, and I knew you 'd save me. You 're my angel! When I dream at night, you 're always hovering over me."

"I 'll come again to-morrow, dearie, when the new doctor has seen you," Barbara answered, as she pressed her hand good-bye.

When they reached the street, Norman asked:

"You knew her before she fell into evil ways?"

"Yes," Barbara answered, with feeling. "She was just a little child of joy and sunlight. She could n't endure the darkness. She loved flowers and music, beauty and love. She hated drudgery and poverty. She tried to work, and gave up in despair. A man came into her life at a critical moment and she broke with the world. She 's been sending all the money she could make the past two years to her mother and four little kids. Her father was killed at work in a mine for a great corporation."

"She can't live, can she?" Norman asked.

"Of course not. I only did this to humour her. She has developed acute consumption — she may not live a month."

Barbara paused.

"I must leave you now — I 'm very tired, and I must sleep a while before I attend the meeting to-night. It has been a great strain on me to-day, this trip with you. How do you like our boasted civilization? Do you think it perfect? Are you satisfied with a system which drives hundreds of thousands of such girls into a life of shame? Are you content with a system which produces three million paupers in a land flowing with milk and honey? Do you like a system which drives thousands to the madness of drink and suicide every year?"

"And to think," responded Norman, dreamily, "that for the past two years of my manhood I 've been writing verses and playing football! Great God!"

"Then from to-day we are comrades in the cause of humanity?" she asked tenderly, extending her hand. His own clasped hers with firm grasp.

"Comrades!"

CHAPTER V

THE ISLAND OF VENTURA

NORMAN had never been a boy to do things by halves. In college, when he went in for football, he made it the one supreme end of life — and won. He incidentally managed to pull through a course in mining engineering. He knew mining by instinct and inheritance from his father. It came easy.

When he had a three months' vacation from football he took up the modelling of a dredge for mining gold from the sands of the beaches. The thing had never been perfected, but after three months' experiment and study he was just on the point of making the castings for the machinery when the football season opened and he dropped such trifling matters for the more serious work of training his men for a successful season. He won the championship and forgot the dredge.

Into the new movement of Socialism he naturally threw his whole personality without reservation. Its daring programme thrilled him. The audacity of its leaders and their refusal to discuss anything less than the salvation of man appealed to every instinct of his nature. He devoured every book on the subject he could find, and in his new-found enthusiasm for humanity accepted as the inspired voice of God their wildest visions of social regeneration.

In his work of charity and organization with Barbara he found everything to confirm and nothing to shake his faith in these theories. When once he caught the idea that all the ills of modern civilization were due directly to the fiendish system of "capitalism" and its "iron law of wages," it was the key which unlocked every mystery of Pain and every tragedy of the Soul. All sin and crime and shame and suffering became the incidents of a social system whose movements were as inexorable as Fate, as merciless as Death. There was but one thing worth talking about, and that was how to destroy modern society, root and branch, and do it quickly, thoroughly and without compromise.

The same daring enthusiasm and capacity for leadership which made him the captain of his football team brought him at once to the front as a Socialist leader. He would have gained this leadership had he been the poorest man among them. It was a gift as his birthright.

But, added to this capacity for daring and successful action, was his wealth and social prestige.

He had cast his lot with a class whose avowed purpose was to destroy all social distinctions, to level all wealth to a common standard. And for this reason in particular he was conspicuous and heroic in the eyes of his Socialist comrades.

He found soon after his entrance into their active councils that the woman known to the world as "The Scarlet Nun," to her associates as "Sister Catherine," was the inspiring brain of their movement in the West. This remarkable woman interested him deeply from their first hour's talk. Born in Poland and educated in Germany, she spoke fluently the Russian, German, French, and English languages. She had led two great strikes of women workers in New York and had been arrested, convicted, and sentenced twice to the penitentiary for exciting riots. To her associates she had always remained a saint and a martyr for their cause.

She had been married before her association with Wolf had begun, ten years ago. Her first husband had been divorced, and her marriage to Wolf had been merely "announced" at a Socialist meeting. And yet the young millionaire had never questioned the sincerity of their devotion or the apparent happiness of their union. He was amazed at her learning, her grasp of affairs, the simplicity and refinement of her manners, and the charm of her conversation.

Wolf he found to be a man of wide reading and deep convictions. As he came in daily contact with these two powerful personalities, and watched the singular zeal with which they devoted themselves to their self-appointed task of destroying modern society, he could not divest himself of the impression that they belonged to a religious order and were leading a crusade, as the monks of the Middle Ages led men and women to die to rescue the tomb of Christ from the desecration of Turk and Saracen.

The woman in particular gave him this impression of religious fanaticism. The apparent simplicity and austerity of her life, the tireless zeal with which she planned and worked for the spread of the gospel of Socialism, to his mind gave the lie emphatically to all the stories he had read of her affairs with men.

The only moments of suspicion about her which ever clouded his mind came with the accidental discovery that she had skilfully managed to throw him and Barbara together for a day. It seemed just a little like the old habit of a scheming mamma angling for the rich young man, and deliberately using the beauty of her daughter as the bait with which to land him in the household.

Yet, when he found himself with Barbara he had always dismissed the thought as absurd. Whatever might be the dimly formed design in the back of the older woman's fancy, her brilliant protégé gave no sign of being her accomplice.

Norman had found Barbara a charming but baffling enigma. She walked through a world of sin and shame, filth and mire, with never a speck on the white of her soul or body. She spoke in the simplest and most direct way of things about which the ordinary girl in society would never dare to utter a word, and yet he took it as a matter of course. He grew to feel that she was a mysterious messenger from the spirit world. Yet when he took her arm and felt its warm round lines soft and thrilling against his own, or the warmth of her lithe body pressing close to his side in some lonely or dangerous spot on their rounds of work, he was brought up sharply against the fact that she was both flesh and spirit. Yet the moment he tried to draw nearer to her inner thoughts, he found her a skilful little fencer, an adept in all the arts of the most delicate and subtle coquetry.

He grew at last, however, to know, with unerring masculine instinct, that with all her brave and frank talk about her "fallen" sisters, she had n't an idea of what their fall really meant. She was as innocent as a child, and when at last she caught the young athlete smiling at one of her apparently frank and learned discussions of the modern degradation of woman, she blushed and became silent. Whereat he laughed, and she became so angry they parted in silence.

Baffled in his efforts to approach Barbara's heart, he threw himself with zeal into the Cause. When two months had been spent in mastering the details of the Socialist programme, in studying its history and the condition of its movement, he called a meeting of the council of the Socialist Club, and fairly took away the breath of the Wolfs and Barbara by the magnitude and audacity of a scheme which he proposed to launch immediately.

He had secured, without consulting any of his associates, an option on a rich, beautiful, and fertile island off the coast of Southern California. It was owned by a corporation which had invested more than a million dollars in its improvement. The enterprise had failed for two reasons — the money had been expended recklessly in the days of the famous land boom, and it had been found impossible to induce labourers to isolate themselves on this lonely spot, sixty miles from the coast of Santa Barbara, with no means of regular connection with the outside world.

His eyes flashing with enthusiasm and his voice ringing with conviction, Norman closed his description of the island of Ventura with a demand for its immediate purchase by the Socialists.

"It can be bought," he declared impetuously, "for $200,000. A million dollars' worth of improvements are already there. I propose that we immediately raise $500,000, buy this island, establish a steamship line, plant a colony of ten thousand Socialists, found the Brotherhood of Man, build a model city, and create a vast fund for the propaganda of our faith."

Barbara's brown eyes danced with excitement, her cheeks flushed, while her little hands clapped approval.

"Good! Good! It's great! It's beautiful! We must do it!" she cried.

Wolf grimly shook his head.

"The idea has failed a hundred times. We must conquer the world by political action — we have the weapon in our hand — manhood suffrage. All colonies fail sooner or later. They are corrupted from outside ——"

"Just so!" Norman interrupted. "But this one you can't reach from the outside. We will own the only means of communication. We will inherit all the advantages of modern civilization with none of its drawbacks. We can demonstrate the truths we hold and from our impregnable Gibraltar send out our missionaries to conquer the world. We will not merely dream dreams and see visions; we will make history. We will prove the God that's in man and establish the fact of his universal brotherhood."

"It's a wonderful idea, comrade!" Catherine exclaimed, with enthusiasm. "I congratulate you! We will accept your plan, and I move that we appoint you our agent vested with full power to collect this fund from the enemy!"

The motion was put and carried unanimously, even Wolf voting for it.

Barbara sprang to Norman's side, and grasped his hand:

"Our feud is over! I forgive you for laughing at me. You are a born leader. You've won your spurs to-night. You will raise this money?"

"As sure as I'm living!" was the firm reply.

CHAPTER VI

THE RED FLAG

NORMAN lost no time in springing his scheme for the establishment of the Socialist colony and headquarters for the propaganda of the new social religion on the island of Ventura. The season he had spent as a reporter gave him the key to the proper launching of a press story which created a profound sensation. It appeared simultaneously in the Sunday editions of all the leading dailies of the Pacific coast, and in forty-eight hours his mail had grown to such proportions that he required two secretaries to assist him in answering it.

He called for a thousand volunteers to join the advance-guard of the coming Brotherhood of Man, each contributing a thousand dollars. He announced a mass meeting and picnic for the Fourth of July, to be held on the big lawn of the Worth country house on the outskirts of Berkeley.

Colonel Worth had readily given his consent to the use of the lawn. He had not tried in any way to interfere with his son's association with the Socialists. He felt sure that in time he would tire of the fad, as he had of football, and in a fatherly way he began to admire the dash and audacity of the boy's plans.

On the morning of the picnic, when Elena expressed her fears of the outcome, the Colonel laughed.

"Don't worry, Elena. He'll come to his senses. It's like a fever. It must run its course. I'm rather proud of the extravagance of his foolishness. A boy who can forget his games and give his life to destroy the foundations of human society and try to rebuild a new world on its ruins — well, there's good stuff in him."

"But if he does something rash?" Elena persisted.

"He won't. With all his extravagance and enthusiasm he's not a fool. I, too, saw visions like that once."

"You, Guardie?"

"Yes, when I was very, very young — a mere boy of thirteen — I joined a colony of Communists."

"I wish I could have seen you at thirteen," Elena cried, with a joyous laugh.

The laugh died suddenly and a frown overspread her face as Norman appeared.

"I want you and Elena to hear our orator to-day, Governor," Norman said, with enthusiasm. "We are going to make it a great day."

"It's already great, my boy — I've just got the news."

"What news?"

The Colonel drew a telegram from his pocket.

"A message from Washington. Sampson and Schley have annihilated the Spanish fleet. Admiral Cervera is a prisoner on board the flagship, and the army is rapidly closing in on the doomed city of Santiago."

He handed the telegram to Norman, who glanced at it in silence and returned it to his father.

"Come to our meeting on the lawn at noon, Governor. We've bigger news than that for you."

"Bigger news?" the older man asked with a quizzical look.

"Yes. A message announcing the dawn of a day when every gun on earth shall be broken to pieces and melted into ploughshares."

The Colonel looked at Norman a moment, smiled, and slowly said:

"I love the young — because I live myself over again in them."

"Then you'll join us to-day?"

"Thanks — no — Elena and I are going to shoot firecrackers — but we won't disturb your crowd. Let them speak to their hearts' content."

The Colonel turned with Elena, and entered the house, which crowned an eminence overlooking the distant bay and city, while Norman hurried down the green sloping lawn to finish the decorations of the speakers' stand.

The crowd had already begun to pour in from Oakland and San Francisco, and more than a hundred delegates from Socialist locals in other cities were expected.

On a little headland which jutted out from the long sloping mountain side on which the lawn was laid out, Colonel Worth had erected a tall steel flag-pole. The big flag which flew from its peak could be seen by every ship that entered or left the bay and for miles on shore in almost every direction.

Around this flag-pole Norman had built the speakers' platform, with every inch of its boards covered with the deep-red bunting symbolic of the Socialist cause. Behind the stand toward the mountains rose a smooth grass-carpeted hillside in semi-circular form, making a natural amphitheatre on which five thousand people might sit in tiers one above the other and distinctly hear every word uttered on the platform.

By noon every inch of this space was packed with a dense crowd of Socialists, their friends, and the curious who had come, drawn by the sensational announcement of the launching of the Socialist colony on the island of Ventura.

In the front row, packed close against the

platform, were a number of famous people —
conspicuous among whom was an author whose
impassioned stories of the coming social upheaval
had resulted in fame for himself and a divorce-suit
by his first wife. His new wife, the "affinity"
who caused the disturbance, sat by his side.

On his left sat a solemn looking poet with bushy,
unkempt hair. He had deliberately chosen the
title "The Bard of Ramcat." The name Ramcat
had been long applied to a shabby section of the
outskirts of San Francisco. Here the poet had
chosen to dwell and sing of social horrors which
existed only in his fertile imagination.

He had won wide fame, however, as the supreme
exponent of the "affinity" theory which has always
been epidemic among thoughtful Socialists. He
coolly informed his wife that he had discovered his
true "affinity" in a woman he had installed as her
guest. The two affinities accompanied the wife
and her child to a steamer for Europe with instructions to obtain a divorce.

The poet married the affinity, and on the birth
of a new son and heir acquired the habit of beating her as a form of relaxation from the strain of
work. Considerable trouble followed, and he
spent a portion of his time in jail. He had once
gone barefooted and bareheaded. But since his
"affinity" marriage he had been compelled for

reasons best known to himself to resume shoe-leather and to buy a hat. Nevertheless he was still a striking-looking figure, seated beside his new wife whose strong, intellectual face won the sympathy of all who saw her.

Just behind him sat an ex-clergyman with whom a rich young woman in his congregation had fallen in love. To avoid trouble, the woman of wealth got him to leave the ministry, and bought him from his wife for a good round sum. He became an apostle of the new gospel of Socialism, and secured a position as a professor of economics. When finally he lost this position by his vagaries, his wife hired a hall and set him up in business as an inspired leader of new thought emancipated from the chains of capitalistic tyranny.

Beside the distinguished ex-clergyman Social-istic apostle sat Professor Otto Schmitt, a famous teacher of economics at a Western university. His supreme passion was hatred of women. His one big book was written to prove that woman has no soul, that she is the mere matter on which man by his will acts, that she is not immoral, but merely non-moral, having never possessed even the rudiments of a moral nature. Schmitt had, therefore, maintained that the entrance of women into competition in the ecomonic world presaged the downfall of man and the utter extinction of humanity. For this reason he had joined the Socialists.

Not three feet away from him sat a thoughtful, elderly, short-haired woman who had written a book on the evolution of woman to prove that woman alone is the original unit of creation, man a superfluous and temporary addition, merely the missing link between woman and the monkey, and in the process of human development the male biped would be eliminated. She demanded equal rights with man, and more besides, and she, too, had joined the Socialists.

Yet through all these ludicrous incongruities there ran the single scarlet thread of social discontent which made them one. In every soul rang the stirring cry:

"Down with civilization! Up with the Red Flag!"

A more remarkable group of men and women could scarcely be gathered together on the face of the earth. But the one mark they all bore, distinctly cut deep in the lines of every face on which character had set its seal, and written large in the restless, nervous personality of the young — they all had a grievance, and though their troubles might come from as many different causes as there were men and women present, they united in one thought:

"Modern civilization must be destroyed!"

Every heart beat with this fiery resolution, and every incongruity melted and faded into insignificance before this consuming belief.

And they had gone about this purpose with a deadly earnestness which meant business. Their political campaigns were merely moments when the captain of their ship cast the lead-line to feel the bottom and find his position with certainty before signalling full speed ahead.

They worked all the year round and every day in every year, from one election to the next. They were mastering the tricks of the demagogue in their appeal to the masses, and they kept everlastingly at it. No man is too high, no man too low, for them to reach for him. They could n't be beaten for they had accepted defeat before they began to fight, and began the next fight before they got up from the ground where they had been knocked down. They had become the one element in American politics to which it was utterly useless to direct any argument of expediency.

The Fourth of July, the Nation's birthday, they were now using to demand its extinction. The fact that our army and navy had just torn the flag of Spain from its last masthead in the Western hemisphere and startled the old world with our sudden advent among the great powers of the earth, stirred in their hearts no emotion save that of contempt. While the souls of millions beat with patriotic pride, they had met to uproot the very ideas from whose soil patriotism sprang into life.

There was no question as to who should be the orator of the day. The fame of Barbara Bozenta had become national from the day of her first speech in San Francisco. Her beauty and eloquence were sufficient to pack any hall at twenty-four hours' notice.

Her delicate face was radiant to-day with unusual elation. She walked with a quick, nervous energy that seemed to lift her whole body into the air. As she ascended the platform and bowed to the tumult of applause, she trembled from head to foot with intensest excitement. As she stood looking over the inspiring scene for a moment, her sensitive nostrils dilated, her brown eyes flashed, and her heart beat with a great throb of personal pride. She had never before faced such an immense throng of excited men and women, and the secret consciousness that she had within her soul the message which would sweep their heartstrings as she willed, lifted her into the clouds.

She felt for the moment that the whole scene

was a tribute to her power. The magnificent house whose windows flashed in the sunlight, the vast lawn carpeted with green and set in dazzling flowers, the emerald waters of the bay, and the spires and domes of the distant city set on its proud hills beyond — all were hers to-day! Her voice had called to their standard the young millionaire whose name was now on every lip. Her voice had inspired his dream of the experiment to be made on the island of Ventura which had called this host together. For one big moment she felt the thrill of conscious creative genius, the pain, the joy, the glory of a positive achievement.

Her eyes suddenly filled with tears, and she sank to her seat with a suppressed sob.

When at last she rose to speak, her whole personality was a quivering battery of resistless emotion. Her voice, low and pulsing with magnetic waves of suppressed feeling, caught and chained the attention of the farthest straggler on the edge of the throng. Instinctively they moved closer. Resistlessly she drew them.

She had not spoken two minutes before she was sweeping the hearts of her hearers. Men and women who had come to laugh or scoff, as well as the young and thoughtless who had drifted with the crowd, were all alike caught in the spell and hung breathless on her words.

Every trick and art of persuasive speech were hers without effort. Scorn, pathos, humour, passion, were of the breath she breathed. At times her eloquence reached the highest conception of its might. It was simple thought packed until it took fire. At such moments scores of men leaped to their feet and shouted. Nothing disconcerted her or changed the swift current of her ideas. She was a master-musician whose hands swept a harp of a thousand strings — every string a throbbing human soul.

What matter if her appeal was to the emotions and not to the intellect? Her purpose was to persuade her hearers. And she did it. Her courage, her beauty, her skill, her utter sincerity, commanded the respect of the strongest man who listened. If their intellects were not convinced, no matter — she carried them with her on a storm of resistless emotion.

Suddenly a thing happened which would have destroyed the total impression of the average speech. Old Methodist John, her pauper protégé, had listened with increasing torture, choking down a hundred "Glorys" as they leaped from his soul until at last he could endure no more. At the climax of one of her impassioned appeals the old man leaped to his feet, rushed in front of the speakers' stand and shouted into the face of the chairman:

"Look here! Look here, now, Wolf! Soup or no soup — Glory hallelujah!"

Barbara alone smiled. The crowd took up his shout, and a thousand voices made the heavens ring with its wild music.

Norman whispered to the old man, who sat down, and Barbara swept on in her impetuous triumph without the lapse of a moment's power. She seized the instant's hush which followed the storm of cheering to fire into the minds of her hearers some of the solid shot of the revolutionary programme.

In a voice which swelled to the clarion note of a trumpet she cried:

"The earth for all the people! This is our demand!

"The machinery of all production and distribution for all the people! This is our demand!

"The collective ownership and control of all industry! This is our demand!

"The elimination of rent, interest, and profit! This is our demand!

"A new social order, a higher civilization, a real republic! This is our demand!

"The end of the hell called war, of poverty

and shame, of cruelty and crime, the birth of freedom, the dawn of brotherhood, the beginning of man! These are our demands! This is Socialism! Is this an idle dream? Have you no faith in your fellow man?

"In the grim prison beyond the bay I found one day a woman convict who was little removed from a fiend. I got permission to hang a beautiful picture in her cell — a picture that set her soul to dreaming, that melted her at last to tears, and transformed the beast within her to a gentle, loving, beautiful, human character.

"I believe in man because he alone possesses this power to look through the window of the soul into the infinite and eternal. Here the world's real battles are fought. Here the world's real work is done. Here cowards run and the brave die. This power to recreate the earth, people it with beauty, and fill it with harmony is your birthright.

"Lo, the day of humanity dawns!

"I preach class consciousness that we may destroy all classes. Class must perish and Man be glorified. Man, whose inhumanity to his fellow man has filled the ages with ashes and tears, is coming forth at last purified by suffering, and we shall see his tears turned to smiles upon the faces of a nobler race.

"Why should we rejoice to-day in the death of

our fellow man? Nations are but the dung-heaps out of which the fair flower of a world-democracy is slowly growing. Truth is not national, it is infinite. France may fight Germany because two titled fools insult each other, but there can be no war between the laboratories of Pasteur and of Koch. Their work is the common heritage of humanity. Who asks if Humboldt was German or English, whether Spinoza was Jew or Gentile, Darwin English or French? A German wrote 'Faust,' a Frenchman set it to immortal music, and an American girl sang it into the hearts of millions. Who cares to know nationalities? The great belong to the democracy of the world. And I swear that your children will still laugh with the soul of Cervantes in spite of the Fourth of July, Santiago, and Manila!

"Why should you fight one another? When called to war by your rulers, let the liberty-loving spirits of the modern world say to their masters:

"'Go and do your own killing — you who have separated us from our brothers and made the earth a slaughter-pen.'

"If you are court-martialed and shot for this act of heroism remember:

"'They never fail who die
In a great cause: the block may soak their gore:
Their heads may sodden in the sun: their limbs
Be strung to city gates and castle walls—

But still their spirit walks abroad.　Though years
Elapse and others share as dark a doom,
They but augment the deep and sweeping thoughts
Which overpower all others, and conduct
The world at last to freedom!' "

A shout of wild applause rent the air as the last note of Byron's immortal song fell from her beautiful lips. And then, in a low, intense voice, she closed her speech with a thrilling appeal for human brotherhood. To Norman, who hung on her lips, the slight girlish figure seemed transformed before their eyes into a radiant messenger of the spirit. And when the sweet womanly tones at last broke and choked into deep-drawn sobs, his soul and body seemed no longer his own. As her last words sank into his heart: "From to-day let each of us swear allegiance to but one flag, the deep-red emblem of human blood, God's sign of universal brotherhood!" Norman leaped to his feet, sprang on the platform, and while the crowd swayed in a frenzy of applause, hauled down the Stars and Stripes and quickly raised the big red standard of Socialism which was thrown across the speaker's table.

And then the great crowd seemed to go mad. Wave after wave of cheering rose and fell, rose and fell, in apparently unending power. Catherine threw her arms around Barbara in a paroxysm of emotion, while the big figure of Wolf towered above them both, shouting and gesturing like a madman. Barbara at last lifted her hand and, as the storm subsided, began the Marseillaise hymn.

The first stirring notes had just swept the audience when the stalwart figure of Colonel Worth suddenly appeared on the platform, his face a blaze of anger, his magnificent figure erect, every nerve and muscle drawn to the highest tension.

He stepped to the edge of the stand, lifted his head, and his voice rang over the crowd like the sudden boom of a cannon:

"Silence!"

He did n't repeat the word.

The singing stopped, and every eye was riveted on the group that stood on the platform.

The Colonel confronted Wolf, and shot his words at him as though from a machine-gun.

"Who lowered that flag?"

A moment of silence followed. The Colonel spoke with increasing rapidity.

"Who lowered that flag? The man who did it must answer to me!"

Some one behind him moved, and the Colonel turned, confronting Norman.

"I did it, Governor," was the quiet answer.

"You?" the father gasped.

"Yes," said the even, firm voice.

"Haul that red rag down and raise the flag

back to its place!" The Colonel's voice was low and thick with rage.

Elena put her hand on his arm and said gently: "Guardie!"

"Will you do it?" he firmly asked, ignoring Elena, and holding Norman with his gaze.

The young man hesitated an instant, met his father's look with a deadly straight stare, and slowly replied:

"I will not."

A smothered cry from Barbara, half joy, half pain, was the only sound that followed, until the Colonel said:

"Then I'll do it for you."

Amid a dead silence he hauled down the red flag, threw it on the floor, boldly stamped on it, made fast the Stars and Stripes, and quickly raised it to the top of its staff. He turned to the crowd, and in clear-cut, sharp tones of command shouted:

"This is my flag, my house, my lawn. Get off it! And do it quick!"

As the crowd hastened away, he turned to Norman:

"You and I must come to an understanding at once, young man," he said, with angry emphasis.

"I'll meet you in the library in thirty minutes," was Norman's firm reply as he led Barbara from the platform and joined the retreating throng.

"Lift the Flag Back to its Place."

CHAPTER VII

FATHER AND SON

THE Colonel paced the floor of his library with increasing anger as he waited the return of Norman. Never in his life had his whole being been so abandoned to incontrollable rage. He had always been a man of fiery temper, but an iron will had held his temper in control.

His most intimate business associates had always found him suave, persuasive, and genial in every hour of trial. Never once had they heard a threat or an idle boast fall from his lips. He had the rare faculty of beating his enemies in a fight in which no quarter was asked or given, and coming out of it with his bitterest foe turned into a friend. This was one of the secrets of his fortune — an instinctive leadership among powerful men.

For the first time he realized that he had challenged the one man in all his personal acquaintance about whose character he knew nothing — his own son. For the first time he realized that they were strangers. He had been absorbed in the big affairs of life. He had taken the boy for granted. Since the death of his mother twelve years ago, Norman had spent most of his time at school.

The Colonel had always been in command. His word had been law for so many years, it brought him up with a disagreeable start to find that the one man with whom his life was bound, and in whom his hopes centred, could dare thus to defy and flaunt his wishes. It was the most disgusting, enraging fact he had ever encountered. The longer he confronted the situation the more furious and blind his anger became.

Elena had timidly entered the room, and stood watching him gravely before she spoke.

"Has he returned from that woman yet?" the Colonel asked with sudden energy.

"No, and I hope he will stay all day," she answered slowly.

"But he won't," the father snapped.

"I'm sure he will not," the girl sighed. "I don't like you to-day, Guardie."

"You, too, side with these fanatics then?"

"No. I hate them — hate everything they say and do and stand for. I loathe the very sight of them. But you were unfair to Norman."

"Unfair? How?"

"You allowed him the widest liberty to do as he pleased, think as he pleased, associate with whom he pleased, and then all of a sudden you sprang on that platform and insulted him before his invited guests."

"How could I dream that he would commit such an act of insane treason before my very eyes?"

"You make no allowance for the spell of Barbara Bozenta's eloquence. I don't like her, but she's a wonderful little woman, and I envy her her power over men."

"I'll end this folly to-day," was the Colonel's firm announcement.

"I'm not so sure," Elena warned.

"I'll show you!"

She came close and laid her hand on the Colonel's arm.

"Will you promise me one thing, Guardie?" she asked, tenderly.

The anger faded from the strong face, and his voice sank low.

"I'm afraid I've never been able to refuse you anything, child. It's on your account, I think, I'm most angry with Norman to-day."

"You promise?" she repeated.

"Yes, what is it?" he said, bending to kiss her smooth, white forehead.

"Promise to put all anger out of your heart and talk to Norman as a father, not as an enemy — won't you?"

"An enemy?" the Colonel slowly asked.

"Yes. I thought you were going to strike him once. It would have been horrible. I never could have forgiven you for that. You 've always been my hero, Guardie — I never saw you give way to anger before. I don't like it. You 'll talk to him lovingly and tenderly as a father, won't you?"

"Yes, dear, for your sake, I will," he answered.

"Then I 'll tell him to come. I asked him to wait outside until I saw you."

She turned and quickly left the room. In a moment Norman entered and stood facing his father.

The Colonel flushed with anger at sight of the insolence with which the younger man calmly surveyed him.

"Well, sir," the father said, at length, "have you nothing to say to me after what has occurred to-day?"

"I was under the impression that you had something to say to me," was the cool answer.

By an effort of will the older man crushed back an angry retort, smiled, and said:

"Sit down, please — I 've a good deal to say to you."

Norman threw himself lazily into a chair, and continued to watch his father with a curious expression of half-amused contempt. The Colonel stood in silence, evidently struggling with his emotions, and feeling for the right word with which to begin.

Norman anticipated him.

"Honestly, now, Governor, just between us, don't you think you were a little bit absurd to-day?"

"Absurd?" his father broke in with rising accent.

"Just a little childish about a piece of red, white, and blue cloth?"

"Perhaps so, my boy," was the answer. "Just about as absurd as you were over the red rag you lifted in its place. Why did you do it?"

"On the impulse of the moment, to express my feeling of contempt for war, and my faith in my fellow man."

"Exactly. So I acted on the impulse of the moment to express my contempt for that crowd of fools and fanatics — my loyalty and faith in my country."

"I can't understand how a man of your age, poise and pride, culture and power, could be so foolish. A sixteen-year-old school-boy on the Fourth of July, yes! But you——"

"Norman," the Colonel interrupted, in even tones, "I'm sorry I've been too busy for us to get acquainted. It's time we began. It may interest you to know that I, too, hate war — learned to hate it long before your Socialist orator was born — learned it in the grim University of Hell — war itself. Socialism has no patent on the hope of universal peace. I am a member of a peace society. I have always believed the Civil War should have been prevented. All the Negroes on this earth are not worth the blood and tears of one year of that struggle. Whether it could have been prevented God alone knows. When it came I volunteered — a drummer-boy at fourteen — and marched to the front beneath the flag you tore down to-day."

"I never thought of that, Governor — honestly, I never did!" the boy exclaimed.

"I went in," the Colonel continued, "with my head full of silly rubbish about the glory of war. When I beat the call to my first charge, and saw the men I knew and loved shot to pieces, and heard their groans and cries for water, I had no more delusions. I worked on the field that night until twelve o'clock, helping the men who were wounded — enemies as well as comrades. I learned the brotherhood of man and the meaning of red blood in the big, tragic school of life, my son. Many a boy in gray, whom I had fought, died in my arms while my heart ached for his loved ones in some far-away Southern home.

"But I knew the war had to be when once it was begun. I was fighting for the flag I loved — and I grew to love it better than life. To you it may be a bit of red, white, and blue bunting; to me it is the symbol of truth and right, liberty and human progress.

"My people in western North Carolina were all slave-holders and loyal to their state, except my father. He hated slavery, loved the Union, and moved on westward before the war. I saw them bury him in the flag you tore down to-day, my boy.

"Many a night I 've lain on the ground looking up at the stars before the dawn of a day of battle and seen visions of that flag flying triumphant in the sky. I 've seen the men who carried it shot down again and again, and another snatch it from their dying grasp and bear it on to victory.

"I grew not only to love it, but to believe in it with all the passionate faith of my soul. I believe in its destiny, in its sublime mission to humanity. The older I 've grown and the more I 've seen of my fellow man, the wider I 've travelled in foreign lands, the deeper has become my conviction that our flag symbolizes the noblest, freest ideal ever born in the soul of man; that we have but to live up to its standard of Liberty, Equality, and Fraternity, and the kingdom of human brotherhood is already here.

"After the war, I joined the regular army, not because I loved war, but because there seemed nothing else for me to do at the time. I was absolutely alone in the world. At twenty-five I was in command of a company on the frontier. I had not been in battle since the end of the Civil War, when suddenly I found myself surrounded by a horde of hostile Indians, and I had to turn my machine guns on them and mow them down. The slaughter was something terrific. As the last charge was made I saw a young squaw retreat in the face of a withering fire, walk backward facing our men, holding a bundle of something behind her body. She fell at last, riddled with bullets. I rode up where she lay, and found the bundle to be a little Indian baby boy. He was unhurt, and stretched out his hand to me in friendly baby greeting. I found the squaw quite dead, and discovered the child was not her own. She was simply trying to save it for the tribe. I took the child and educated him. But he went back to the free life of the plains. I found him again, and made him the gamekeeper of our mountain preserves."

"You mean Saka?" Norman asked.

"Yes. That night as I lay in my tent I saw war as it is — a hideous, savage nightmare. From that moment I hated the service, hated its iron laws of discipline, its cruel machinery devised for suppressing the individuality of its members. I saw that night a larger vision of life. I made up my mind to create, not to kill — to build up, not to tear down. I left the army and mastered mining.

"Your leather-lunged agitators say that I stole my millions from the earnings of the men who worked for me. A more stupid lie was never uttered. I invented improved mining machinery. I made deserts blossom and gave employment to thousands of men who could n't think for themselves. I did their thinking for them, and set their tasks. I have made millions, and have added tens of millions to the wealth of the West."

"If labour is the creator of all wealth can one man ever earn a million dollars?" Norman interrupted.

"Manual labour is not the creator of wealth. The brain which conceives is the creator of wealth. The hand which executes these plans is merely the automaton moved by a superior power."

"Yet nothing could be accomplished without it," persisted Norman.

His father lifted his hand with a gesture of command.

"We'll not discuss the theory of Socialism to-day, my boy. I grant you have plausible arguments which skilful demagogues are using with more and more efficiency. I don't object to your study of this subject. I'm rather pleased at the serious turn your energies have taken. What I do object to is your continued association with the kind of people who made up that crowd to-day — people who make the agitation of the revolutionary programme of the Socialists a daily profession, people who are seeking to destroy modern civilization itself."

"You will have to come down to earth, Governor," Norman said, "in your indictment of these people. The time has gone by when you can scare anybody with a few high-sounding phrases. If modern civilization is rotten, it ought to be destroyed, and who cares if it is?"

"The issue between us, my boy," the Colonel continued, gravely, "is not an academic one. It is not open to discussion. Some of the people you are associating with have criminal records. If they continue their present wild harangues they will be shot down like dogs in the streets. I cannot afford to have my name even under the suspicion of sympathy for them, through you. Do you understand me?"

"I think I do," Norman replied, holding his father's steady gaze.

"You are my son and the heir of my fortune. But you must remember that I am the master of this establishment."

"I am aware of that fact, sir," the boy replied, in cold tones.

"I trust that it will not be necessary, then, for me to repeat to you my first positive order — that you will immediately sever your connection with the Socialist Club, and never again appear in public or private with the three people who were on that platform to-day."

"It will not be necessary for you to repeat your order," the young athlete replied, with a curious smile and a slight tightening of the lips.

"I thought as much."

Norman laughed, and the Colonel's eyes began to blaze.

"What do you mean, sir?" he sternly asked.

"That it will be unnecessary for you to repeat your order, for the very simple reason that I'm a man. I've the right to do my own thinking, and I propose to do it."

With a quick stride the Colonel confronted the young rebel, his breath quick and laboured, his face aflame with unbridled rage.

"You dare thus to defy my wishes?"

"If you put it that way, yes."

The Colonel stepped to the door and opened it.

"You will obey my order or get out of this house never to enter it again. Take your choice!"

"You mean it?" the younger man asked, with sullen emphasis.

"Exactly what I say," was the cold reply.

Norman turned without a word, seized his hat, and left the room. As he reached the end of the corridor, and placed his hand on the front door, his father's voice rang out suddenly:

"Norman!"

He paused, and looked back without taking his hand from the knob.

"You can't be such a fool!" the Colonel cried.

"It looks that way, Governor!"

He opened the door, softly closed it, and was gone.

CHAPTER VIII

THROUGH THE EYES OF LOVE

NORMAN'S break with his father created a sensation. The flag episode, coming on the Fourth of July and at the very hour when the guns of the forts were thundering their celebration of the fleet's victory at Santiago, presented the dramatic contrast which stirred the indignation of the public to unusual depths. The morning papers devoted from four to five columns to the story. The remarkable speech of Barbara Bozenta was reported in full, with a sketch of her life, interspersed with portraits of the Wolfs, of Norman, Elena, his father, the palatial home on Nob Hill, and the country estate where the stirring little drama had been played.

The Socialist cause received a tremendous impetus. The very violence of the editorial assaults on their programme reacted in their favour. Thousands of men who did not know the meaning of the word Socialism began to read and think and discuss its principles. Their meetings were crowded, and the fame of the little brown-eyed Joan of Arc became so great it was no longer possible for her to pass through the streets without an escort.

All sorts of stories about the relations of the famous millionaire and his son filled the air. Some were printed, others were vague rumours. A sensational paper published the story that they had actually come to blows, and had fought a duel in the big library which might have ended fatally for one or both but for the timely interference of Colonel Worth's ward, Elena Stockton.

Norman became at once the hero of the Socialist's cause. His appearance at a meeting was the signal for pandemonium to break loose. He secured employment on a sensational daily paper, and his signed articles were made a feature.

Colonel Worth was so enraged over the vulgar notoriety with which the incident had overwhelmed him that he denied himself to all callers, refused to speak to a reporter or to allow a word to be uttered in confirmation or denial of any stories printed or rumoured.

He issued orders that Norman's name should never again be spoken in his house.

When he made this announcement to Elena her full, red lips, quivered and she looked at him reproachfully.

"I mean it, Elena," he said, sternly.

The girl spoke in tenderness.

"I don't believe you, Guardie. It is n't like you at all. I 'll not mention his name to a servant, but I will to you."

"I don't want to hear it!"

"That 's because you know you 've done a great wrong."

"I accept the responsibility. It 's done, and that 's the end of it."

"Nothing ends until it ends right, Guardie," spoke the soft, even voice.

"I know it 's hard on you, dear," the Colonel responded, with feeling. "It was for your sake I made the issue. If he has turned from you for a loud-mouthed vulgar agitator, he 's not worth a thought. Forget that he lives. I 'm going to leave my fortune to you."

"I don't want it at the price, Guardie," she replied, slipping her arm around his neck and resting her head on his shoulder. "I could n't be happy with such a fortune. What you 've done hurts me more than it hurts Norman."

"Yes, yes. I know that you love him, child, but your happiness could not be found among a crowd of criminals and revolutionists."

"I 'm not thinking of myself," was the low

response as she withdrew from his arms, "I was thinking of you."

"Of me?"

"Yes. You've broken my idol. To me you were the one perfect man in the world. I didn't know you. I didn't know that you were hard and cold and cruel and selfish and proud."

"I'm not, Elena."

"You allowed Norman to drift into any crazy theory that might strike his fancy. And the moment he fails to agree with your views you turn like a madman and drive him into the streets."

"He went of his own accord. I gave him his choice."

"And I admire his pluck. It was a manly thing to do."

"It was the act of a fool."

"Yet, you know, Guardie, in your heart of hearts you admire him for it. He showed you that he was made of the same stuff as his father."

The Colonel scowled, and the girl took courage.

"I'm going to meet him this evening ——"

"I forbid it!"

"You can't help it," she cried, as the tears slowly gathered. "I'm going to tell him you wish to see and talk with him again."

"On one condition only—his absolute obedience to my wishes."

"I love him all the more for defying you — love him better than I ever did in my life. And — and, Guardie — I don't love you any more. You are cruel and unjust."

With a sob she turned and left the room.

CHAPTER IX

A FADED PICTURE

ELENA'S tears had shaken the Colonel's confidence in his position as nothing else could possibly have done. Since she had finished her course in college two years before, and he had come in daily contact with her strong personality, a most intimate and perfect sympathy had grown between them. He had never before known her intuitive judgment to be wrong. Her impressions of character especially he had found singularly accurate, her sense of right and her good taste nearly perfect.

He retired to his room at night with a deep sense of uneasiness. His anger had cooled, and in its stead a feeling of depression slowly settled. From every nook and corner came memories of the boy he had driven from his door. His pictures hung on the walls and stared at him from every piece of furniture on which a frame could be placed. He had learned photography as a pastime years before the kodak was invented, and most of the pictures he had taken himself.

One photograph in particular, which stood by the

clock on the mantel, set in a heavy frame of hammered gold, which he had made himself from the product of his first mine, riveted and held his attention. His first impulse was to tear these pictures all down and throw them in the fire. He had picked this one up first, to carry out his furious impulse, but something held his hand and he placed it back in its old place with the grim exclamation:

"No! It's the act of a coward. I've got to live with my memories — or surrender at once."

Again and again his eye came back to this picture. He had taken it twenty-three years ago in a little bedroom in a dirty hotel of a desolate, God-forsaken mining town in Nevada. How well he remembered it! He was poor then, and had just begun the first big fight of his life for wealth and power. The boy was four weeks old, and he had insisted on taking the picture of the mother with the baby in her arms. He had carefully posed her, standing by the window looking down into the child's upturned face. It had turned out a remarkable likeness of both — the young mother's face wreathed in smiles, tender and frail and happy, with the great joy of the dawn of motherhood shining in her eyes.

He looked at it long and tenderly. And, as a

thousand memories of life crowded his soul, he suddenly exclaimed:

"God in heaven! What does she say to-day if she knows what I 've done?"

His eyes blinked, and the tears blinded them.

He kissed the picture and buried his face in his hands as a sob of anguish shook his frame.

"The girl's right. My boy's my boy after all. I 'm wrong!"

CHAPTER X

SON AND FATHER

WHEN the Colonel had greeted Elena at breakfast next morning he quietly asked:
"You met Norman ?"

"Yes."

"I shall be glad to see him when he comes."

Elena threw her arms impulsively around his neck.

"Now you 're a darling! Now you 're big and strong and good and great again — and I love you."

The Colonel stroked her hair slowly, and asked with a smile:

"What time is he coming ?"

"He 's not coming." Elena laughed.

"Not coming ?" the colonel repeated blankly.

"No.   You 're going to see him."

"Indeed!"

"You see, Guardie, he is a chip off the old block."

"It begins to look like he 's the whole block," the Colonel remarked, dryly.

"Can you blame him after the way you acted ?"

"I can't say I do, much. I like a boy of spirit ——"

"And individuality — that's your own pet idea Guardie.''

The Colonel was silent a moment.

"Yes. I like his grit. Where will I find him?"

"At his desk at work in the newspaper office.''

"I 'll call him up and make an appointment."

The Colonel seized the telephone, called the newspaper office, and asked for Norman. He waited for several minutes before any one reached the 'phone. He scarcely recognized the short, sharp business accent of Norman's voice:

"Well, well, what is it?"

The Colonel cleared his throat.

"Here! Here! Get a move on you — what's the matter — I 'm in a hurry!"

"This is your father, Norman ——"

Get off the wire or quit your kiddin'— what do you want?"

His father laughed.

"I beg your pardon, Governor, honestly I did n't recognize your voice until you laughed. I 'm awfully glad to hear it again. What can I do for you?"

"Well, I must say I like your impudence. What can *you* do for me? I want to see you right away. Shall I call at your office?"

A pause ensued, followed by audible smiles at both ends of the wire.

"Of course not, sir. It seems a long time since I left home but I 've not forgotten the way. I 'll come over as soon as I can leave my desk."

Two hours later he entered the library with a boyish laugh and grasped his father's hand.

The Colonel pressed it with deep tenderness.

"You must forgive me, boy. I was n't fair to you the other day."

Norman tried to laugh, and stammered awkwardly:

"Well, when I hear a man of your age and experience say a thing like that, Governor, I begin to fear I 'm not quite as big as I thought I was."

"Then we 're both in the right mind now, to begin all over again, are we not?"

"It 's with you, sir," was the quick reply.

"Suppose I can convince you that you have entered on a mistaken mission — that your programme is foolish, impossible, and dangerous?"

"Do it, and I 'll join you in trying to put an end to Socialism."

"Before I begin, let me ask you a very personal question."

"As many as you like, Governor," was the frank response.

"Are you mixed up in any way personally with the young woman who spoke here that day?"

"We 're comrades in the cause of humanity — that 's all."

"You 're sure that it is not her personal influence over you that has made you a Socialist?"

"Only in so far as she has made me think and feel."

"You have not made love to her?"

"Certainly not. I 'm engaged to Elena."

"Then it ought to be easy for us to understand each other. Come down out of the clouds of theory now, and tell me exactly how you are going to save humanity, and let 's see if we can't work together for the same end. A great purpose like yours ought not to separate father and son — you can't defend such platitudes as this, for example, which one of your orators got off last night — listen!"

The Colonel took the morning paper from the table and read:

"Remember in this supreme hour that capitalism has you and your loved ones by the throats, is stealing your substance, draining your veins, and reducing you inch by inch to the potter's field. Every sweating den cries out to you as from the depths of hell to gird up your loins and march forth in one solid phalanx to strike the blow that shall sound the knell of capitalistic despotism, and set the star of hope in the skies of the despairing and dying thousands of your class who are at the mercy of the vampires of soulless wealth. How long shall capitalism be allowed to work its devastation, spread its blighting curse, destroy manhood, debauch womanhood, and grind the flesh and blood and bone of childhood into food for Mammon?"

The Colonel paused.

"Such appeals to passion can only end in riot, bloodshed, and prison bars. You don't write such rot as that yourself, and yet the men you are following preach it."

"I'm not following just now, Governor — I'm trying to direct this tremendous impulse, this enthusiasm for humanity, called Socialism, into a practical experiment that will demonstrate the truths of their faith, and from this white city of a glorified human life send out our missionaries to conquer the world. Give me ten thousand earnest men and women on the island of Ventura, isolated from contact with the corruption of the outside, and I'll show you a miracle more wonderful than if they had risen from the dead."

"And what are the foundations on which you propose to build this heaven on earth?"

"Squarely on these principles: From every man

according to his ability; to every man according to his needs; and to every child born the right to laugh and play and grow to a strong manhood and womanhood. We are not civilized so long as there is one child sobbing to be freed from the tomb of the modern workshop, so long as there is one man willing to work and not able to find it, so long as there is one soul striving upward who is crushed to earth, so long as one man lives in idleness and luxury while his neighbour starves, so long as there's one spot of this earth on which a man lives by tearing the bread from the lips of another."

"Hasn't your imagination been caught by beautiful phrases, my boy?" asked the father. "In your new State of Ventura you will give to each man according to his needs?"

"Yes."

"And who will decide how much each one needs — the man who feels the need or the state?"

"The state, in the last resort."

"Exactly. And who will determine how large the service required of each man? Who will decide the question of ability?"

"The state, of course."

"Are you not cutting out a pretty big job for the state, remembering that the state is nothing more or less than a lot of ordinary second-rate politicians named Tom, Dick, and Harry, who individually or collectively have n't as much sense as you or I?"

"In the new world it will be different."

"Then you are going to import a new breed of men and women?"

"No, we will simply give the God in man a chance to be."

"But how about the beast that 's in man — the elemental instinct to fight and kill — to take the woman he desires by the force of his hands and muscle?"

"When man is free and strong and happy he can have no motive to kill or play the beast."

"That remains to be seen, my boy! Your assertion does not change the nature of man. Another problem in your scheme I can't solve is wages."

"We will abolish wage slavery."

"Yes, yes, I know; but man must work — all men must work in your new state?"

"Certainly."

"And the man who refuses to work?"

"Will be made to work according to his ability."

"Just so. We live under the wage system now — the system of free contract by which labourer

and employer agree. Under your system contract would be abolished, and men would do what
they are *told* to do — a system of *command*
instead of *contract* — is it not so?"

"I should say just the opposite. Men are
forced to work now at tasks they loathe and for
pay that is insufficient. Under our state they
would be free to choose the work for which they
are fitted."

"And suppose they all choose one job?"

"The state would assign their work in the last
resort."

"There you are, once more, bowing down to
the same Tom, Dick, and Harry. And you
cannot see that Socialism would impose on man
the most colossal system of slavery, the most
merciless because the most impersonal, the world
ever saw?"

"No, I cannot. Give me a chance on one
spot of earth free from the corruption of your
present system, and I'll show you that man is a
child of God, that deep in every human soul is
planted the sense of brotherhood, justice, and
human fellowship."

"And you will abolish private property?"

"Except what each man earns or makes for
himself."

The Colonel laughed aloud.

"Can he earn a wife, or make one for himself?"

"No; nor own one as a slave."

"You can never abolish private property, my boy, so long as any man has the right to say, 'This woman is mine.' The home is the basis of modern civilization. If you destroy it the home will not survive. If the home survives it will kill Socialism. The two things can't mix."

Norman laughed.

"And you think capitalism is building ideal homes with its drudgery that kills woman — its poverty that starves the man and drives the girl to a life of shame?"

"Our conditions are not ideal, my son. But they are growing better with each generation. Because all homes are not ideal, you propose to abolish the institution. There are ten million homes in America. Perhaps a million of them are unhappy. Can we mend matters by destroying them all?"

"Socialism proposes to build the highest ideal of home ever seen on earth, founded on love — and only love."

The Colonel smiled sadly.

"I see I'm too late. You've got it bad. Socialism is a contagious disease, imported from the old world — a brain disease, the result of centuries of wrong and oppression. Its reasons for existence in this country are purely imaginary. If it were possible for you to build the new State of Ventura of which you dream ——"

"Dream! We are going to do it, I tell you, Governor! We have a hundred thousand dollars already pledged. We hold to-morrow night a great mass-meeting at which five thousand Socialists will be present. Four hundred thousand dollars more will buy the island and give a capital of three hundred thousand with which to begin."

"Then I can't persuade you to give up this madness?" the Colonel asked, tenderly.

"It's my life," Norman answered firmly.

The father slipped his arm around the tall, strong figure.

"All right! Remember now, from this moment on, one thing is settled for good and all. My boy's my boy, right or wrong, good or bad, wise or foolish ——"

The Colonel's voice broke, and his grip tightened.

Norman looked out of the window, blinked his eyes, and said in low tones:

"I understand, sir!"

CHAPTER XI

THE WAY OF A WOMAN

AS ELENA entered the library the two men fell suddenly apart as though ashamed of the weakness of affection before a woman.

The girl pretended not to have seen, but her face was radiant.

The Colonel paused as he turned to leave the room:

"You will keep up your newspaper grind, my boy?" he asked.

"No. I'll jump at the chance to do the big thing. I'll give my whole time to it."

"Well, I suppose you're right. The way to do a thing is to do it."

As the father passed Elena he softly whispered:

"Your face shines like an angel's!"

"I am very happy," was the low answer.

Norman hastened to her side, and seized both her hands.

"I owe this to you, my stately queen."

"He would have come to the same conclusion himself. I only hastened it a little by a suggestion," she replied.

"I have my own idea about the way you expressed it," he said with a jolly laugh. "Look here, Elena, I hope you don't believe that I have been disloyal to you in my association with Barbara Bozenta?"

The girl straightened her superb figure, and broke into a laugh of mingled humour and irony.

"Well, I 've a confession to make, Norman. I 've been disloyal to you."

"You — disloyal — to me!" he gasped.

"Yes. I 've felt of late as though you were a big, sick baby on my hands, and I 've grown tired of the charge."

"Well, upon my soul!" he exclaimed.

"Our engagement is at an end. "

"Elena!"

"I 'll keep your beautiful ring" — she touched it affectionately — "for the memories that will always bind us as brother and sister. Besides, it will deceive your father for a while. He has enough to worry him just now."

Before Norman could pull himself together, or utter a protest, she had turned and left him gasping with astonishment.

CHAPTER XII

A ROYAL GIFT

NORMAN resumed his place in his father's home and began a systematic, persistent, and enthusiastic campaign to raise the funds to purchase the island of Ventura and establish the ideal Commonwealth of Man.

On the day of the big mass-meeting of Socialists, who had gathered from every state of the Golden West, Elena found her guardian seated alone on the broad veranda overlooking the Bay of San Francisco. A look of deep trouble clouded his strong face.

"You are worried?" she said, seating herself by his side.

"Yes, dearie," was the moody answer.

"Over Norman's meeting?"

"Yes. The boy's set his heart on this big foolish enterprise. His failure is a certainty. I don't know what may follow."

"You are sure he can't raise the money?"

"Absolutely. The disappointment will be a stunning blow to his pride."

"You know that if he did succeed in raising the

money, and establishing his brotherhood of man, the scheme would end in failure?"

"As clearly as I know I am living."

"Would you be sorry if the dream should be realized?"

"On the other hand, I'd shout for joy to find the human race capable of such a miracle."

Elena gently touched his hand. "Then, Guardie, there's but one thing to do," she said, with a deep, spiritual look in her blue eyes.

"What?"

"Give Norman a round million dollars to make the experiment."

The Colonel looked at her in amazement, and suddenly sprang to his feet, pacing the floor with feverish steps. He stopped at last before the girl and studied her.

"Don't let Norman know who gave the money," she continued. "It will be a big, noble, beautiful thing to do — and — it will save him."

"What a wonderful woman you are, Elena!"

He paused and looked at her steadily. "I'm going to do it!"

When Norman returned at midnight from the mass-meeting his face was flushed and his eyes sparkled.

"It's done, Governor! It's done!" he fairly shouted.

"You mean the half million was subscribed?" the Colonel asked.

"Yes, and more!" he went on, excitedly. "We have succeeded beyond my wildest hopes. We had subscriptions for a hundred thousand. Fifty thousand more was subscribed at the meeting by the delegates, and just as we were about to adjourn Judge Clark, a famous lawyer, rose and announced the gift of a round million to the cause by a group of friends whose names he refused to make known."

"And what happened?" Elena asked.

"It's hard to tell exactly. The first thing I did was to jump over three rows of seats, grab the lawyer, and yell like a maniac. We carried him around the room, and shouted and screamed until we were hoarse. The scene was indescribable. Strong men fell into each other's arms and cried like children."

"And you could get no hint of the identity of the men who gave the money?" Elena inquired.

"Not the slightest. The deed of gift was made to me through the lawyer as trustee. I don't like one or two conditions, exactly, but it was no time to haggle over details."

"What were the conditions?" Elena interrupted, with a glance at the Colonel.

"That the title to the island of Ventura should be vested in me personally for two years. And five hundred thousand dollars should remain a fund in my hands as trustee to administer its income for the same period. At the end of one year, or of two, I may transfer the whole to the Brotherhood, or reconvey it to the original donors. I think it gives too much power into one man's hands — but I'll hold it a sacred trust."

The young enthusiast's face glowed with thrilling purpose, and his eyes were shining with unshed tears, as he laid his hand on his father's shoulder and exclaimed:

"Ah! Governor, you did n't have faith enough in your fellow man! You said it could n't be done!"

"I congratulate you, my son," the Colonel gravely said, "and I wish for you the noblest success."

"There 's no such word as fail." Norman cried. "No sleep for me to-night! I return to the Socialist Club for a celebration. I just came to tell you personally of our triumph. The deed is done, and the Brotherhood of Man is a thrilling fact!"

With swift, joyous stride he threw himself into the hall and bounded down the steps.

"Suppose after all, Guardie, he should succeed?" Elena exclaimed.

"They'll start with many things in their favour," the Colonel responded. "The island of Ventura is said to be the most fertile and beautiful spot of earth in the West. No adverse influences can reach them from without. Five thousand men and women, inspired by a sublime faith in themselves, may under such conditions surprise us. If Socialism is possible on an island of a hundred thousand acres, it's possible on a hundred thousand square miles, and its faith will conquer the world. We'll give them two years before we visit them, and see what happens."

"Suppose they do succeed!" Elena repeated, musingly.

CHAPTER XIII

THE BURNING OF THE BRIDGES

THE success which attended the launching of the new Brotherhood of Man with its million-dollar endowment fund was phenomenal.

The announcement that the books were ready for the enrollment of the pioneer group of two thousand who should locate the enterprise on the island of Ventura brought twenty-five thousand applicants.

The first shock Norman's faith in man received was to collide with the army of cranks who came in troops to join. Every creed of Christendom, every cult of the heathen world, every ism of all the philosophies of the past and the present came in droves. They got into arguments with one another in the waiting-rooms of the Socialist headquarters, and sometimes came to blows. Each conceived the hour for establishing his own particular patent for saving the human race had come. It was an appalling revelation to Norman to find how many of these schemes were at work in the brains of people who were evidently incapable of taking care of themselves.

The first week he attempted to hear each one with courtesy and sympathy. But after wasting six days in idiotic discussions of preposterous schemes he was compelled to call on the Wolfs for advice

Both Wolf and his wife had begun to call Norman "Chief" from the moment of their first burst of enthusiasm over the gift of the million. At times the young dreamer looked at the massive face of the older man with a touch of suspicion at this sudden acceptance of his premiership. And yet both Wolf and Catherine (she insisted that he call her Catherine) seemed so utterly sincere in their admiration, so enthusiastic in their faith in his ability, they always disarmed suspicion. Catherine's repeated explanation of this faith when Norman halted or hesitated was always flattering to his vanity, and yet perfectly reasonable.

"My boy, we take off our hats to you! A man can't do the impossible unless he tries. We did n't try. You did. The trouble with Herman, and with every man of forty, is that he loses faith in himself. We get careful and conservative. We lack the dash and fire and daring of youth. I envy you. I salute you as the inspired leader of our Cause — you 've done the impossible! And you 've just begun. We can only hope to help you with our larger experience."

At the end of a week of futile and exhausting palaver with this army of cranks who infest the West, Wolf, carefully watching his opportunity, turned to Norman and said:

"I 've been waiting for you to see things a little more clearly before I say something to you — I think it 's time."

"What is it ?" the young leader asked.

Wolf hesitated a moment as if feeling his way.

"Something he should have said sooner." exclaimed Catherine.

"There 's but one way, comrade. Kick these fools into the street!"

"But don't we begin to weaken the moment we do a thing like that ? We accept the brotherhood of man ——"

"Of man, yes," the old leader broke in, "but these are not men — they are what might have been had they lived in a sane world. They are the results of the nightmare we call civilization. The kindest thing you can do for a crank is to kill him. You are trying to do what God Almighty never undertook — to make something out of nothing. You know, when he made Adam he had a ball of mud to start with."

"I 'm afraid you 're right," Norman agreed.

"When the Brotherhood is established with picked men," Catherine added, "we can take

in new members with less care. Now it is of
the utmost importance that we select the pioneer
group of the best blood in the Socialist ranks —
trained men and women who believe with passionate faith what you and I believe."

"Then do it," Norman said, with emphasis.
"I put you and Wolf in charge of this first roll.
I've more important work to do in organizing
the business details of the enterprise."

A look of joy flashed from Wolf's gray eyes
into the woman's as he calmly but quickly
replied:"

"I'll do the best I can."

"You ought to know by name every true
Socialist on the Coast," Norman added.

"I do, comrade, and I'll guarantee the pioneer
group."

"Let all applicants for membership hereafter
pass your scrutiny," were his final orders.

He rose from his desk with a sigh of relief as
Barbara entered the room, her cheeks flushed
with joy, her eyes sparkling with excitement from
the ovation she had just received from the crowd
which packed the corridor.

His first impulse was to ask her to accompany
him to the country, rest and play for a day.
His heart beat more quickly at the thought, but as
the question trembled on his lips, his eyes rested

on Wolf's shaggy head bending over the piles of papers on his desk, and a grim fear shadowed his imagination. Elena's laughter suddenly echoed through his memory. He recalled his father's questions. A frown slowly settled on his brow, and a firm resolution took shape in his mind.

"No woman's spell to blind your senses! Clear thinking, my boy! You 're on trial before the man who gave you life. You 're on trial before the men whose faith gave you a million dollars to put you to the test. Success first, and then, perhaps, the joy of living!"

Barbara felt the chill of a sudden barrier between them, and looked at him with a little touch of wounded pride.

He merely nodded pleasantly and hurried from the room.

He gave his whole energies at once to the larger business of the enterprise. The title to the property was searched with the utmost thoroughness and found to be perfect. Enormous sums of money had been spent on the island by the bankrupt wild-cat real-estate company which had bought it in for improvement and exploitation. They had built a magnificent hotel with accommodations for one thousand five hundred guests, had planted vineyards, established a winery planted vast orchards of plums, apricots, olives, peaches, and oranges, built flour mills, an ice factory, and had started a number of mining and manufacturing enterprises. When the bubble burst the company was bankrupt and the lawyers got the rest. A careful inventory showed to Norman that they had acquired a property of enormous value. The improvements alone had cost $1,250,000, and they were worth twice that sum now to the colony.

He chartered a corporate society, known as "The Brotherhood of Man," for the purpose of legalizing the new social State of Ventura when it had passed the experimental stage and he could surrender to it the title and money held in trust under the deed of gift. Two hundred thousand dollars was paid in cash for the island, and the remaining capital held for work. A steamer was purchased to serve the colony by plying between the island, Santa Barbara, and San Francisco.

The Wolfs advised Norman that no mail service be asked or permitted.

"The reasons are many, comrade," the old leader urged. "The first condition of success in this work is the complete isolation of the colony from outside influences. If modern civilization is hell, you can't build a heaven with daily communication between the two places."

"Every man and woman who enters," Catherine added, "must sign a solemn contract to remain five years, enlist as soldier, and communicate with the outside world only by permission of the authority of the Brotherhood."

"I see," laughed Norman. "I must have the Czar's power to examine suspected mail if treason or rebellion threatens."

"Exactly," cried Wolf.

"A large power to put in one man's hands," Norman protested.

"There's not a man or woman going to that island who would n't trust you with life, to say nothing of a mail pouch," Catherine declared, with a look of genuine admiration.

"You think such drastic measures to prevent communication with the outside world will be needed?" Norman argued.

"Let us hope not," Wolf quickly replied. "But it's better to be on the safe side. The history of every experiment made in Socialism by the heroes and pioneers of the cause in the past shows that failure came in every case from just this source. We will start under the most favourable conditions ever tried. Our island will be a little world within itself. Cut every line of possible communication with modern competitive society, and we can prove the brotherhood of man a living fact. Open our experiment to the lies and slanders of our enemies from without, and they can destroy us before the work is fairly begun. Our colony would be overrun with hostile reporters from the capitalist press, for example ——"

"You 're right," exclaimed Norman.

"Let every volunteer enlist in the service of humanity for five years," repeated Catherine, "agreeing to hold no communication with the world. Make that agreement one impossible for them to break, and our success is as sure as that man is made in the image of God. All we ask is a chance to prove it without interference."

"I agree with you," cried Norman, at last. "Five years' service, with every bridge burned behind us — we 'll fight it out on that line."

A look of triumph came from beneath Wolf's shaggy brows as his eyes rested again on the smiling madonna-like face of the woman by his side.

CHAPTER XIV

THE NEW WORLD

ON A beautiful Sunday morning in May, 1899, the steamship *Comrade* slowly swept through the Golden Gate with two thousand enthusiastic Socialists crowding her decks, shouting, cheering, laughing, crying, singing their joy and faith in the new world of human brotherhood for which they had set sail.

The flag of the republic flew from her stern because the law of the port of entry required it. But from her huge prow rose a slender steel staff, above the tips of her funnels and masts, on which flew the blood-red ensign of Socialism, while from every masthead huge red steamers fluttered in the sky.

At noon on the following day the eager eyes of the pioneers sighted the island of Ventura. At first a tiny white and blue spot on the horizon, and then slowly out of the sea rose its majestic outlines, until at last the ship drew in so close to the towering mountains of its shore line the colonists could almost touch the stone walls with their hands.

The captain was evidently at home in the sparkling blue waters which rolled lazily against the perpendicular cliffs.

Norman had climbed over the piles of freight, cordage, and anchors, and taken his stand beside the flagstaff on the ship's prow, his soul enraptured with the thrilling adventure on which he had embarked.

He had made two trips to the island before, but never had he seen it rise from the sea in such matchless glory as to-day.

Far up in the sky loomed the mountain peaks still covered with snow, while the rich hills and valleys to the southward rolled laughingly in their robes of green.

Five miles down the coast the ship turned her nose inshore, and slowly ploughed her way through a narrow channel which opened between two hills. She quickly cleared the channel and rounded another headland, when a shout rang from her decks. Straight before them, across a beautiful landlocked bay, which formed a perfect harbour, rose the huge hotel, the home of the Brotherhood. The central building was crowned by two tall towers, and the long wings which stretched toward the sea pierced the skyline with a dozen minarets of quaint Moorish pattern. From the flagpole on the lawn, from each graceful tower and each shining sun-kissed minaret, flew the scarlet ensign of Socialism.

When the ship swept in alongside the pier the building loomed from its hilltop higher apparently than the mountain range behind it.

Barbara clapped her hands as she ran to Norman's side.

"Look! Look at those flags! Are n't they glorious? Nobody will haul them down here, will they?"

Norman lifted his eyes and looked in silence for a moment. A stiff breeze was blowing from the southeast, and the two huge banners of scarlet stood straight from their staffs on the towers and seemed to fill the sky with quivering flame.

"Glorious!" he said, at last. "They speak the end of strife, the dawn of love and human brotherhood!"

The Wolfs had preceded them to the colony with a select band of enthusiasts, stored the first supplies, and set the place in order to receive as welcome guests the first shipload of pioneers.

When the throng of joyous, excited comrades had landed, they formed in line and marched up from the pier. The wide, white, smooth road led through a wilderness of flowers which had grown in wild profusion since they had been abandoned two years before. The Wolfs led the procession, with Barbara and Norman by their side.

When they reached the big circle of scarlet geraniums in the centre of the floral court between the two wings of the great building they stopped, and Catherine began in her clear, thrilling soprano voice the Marseillaise hymn. The pioneers crowded around her tall, commanding figure and sang with inspired emotion. Every heart beat with high resolve. The heaven of which they had dreamed was no longer a dream. They were walking its white, shining streets. Their souls were crying for joy in its dazzling court of honour. The old world, with its sin and shame, its crime and misery, its hunger and cold, its greed and lust, its cruelty and insanity, had passed away, and lo! all things were new. The very air was charged with faith and hope and love. A wave of religious ecstasy swept the crowd. They called each by their first names. Strong men embraced, crying "Comrade!" through their tears. The older ones had made allowances for the glowing accounts of the island. They expected some disillusioning at first. Yet their wildest expectations were far surpassed. Such beauty, such grandeur, such wealth of nature, such magnificence of equipment, were too good to be true, and yet they were facts.

The island of Ventura was enchanted. The impression it gave each heart of the certainty of success was the biggest asset of real wealth with which the colony began its history.

CHAPTER XV

FOR THE CAUSE

DURING the first enchanted days every man woman and child entered the strange new system with a determination to see only its beauty, its truth, its sure success. Service was the order of the day. Men who had never before worked with their hands asked the privilege of the hardest tasks.

The whole colony swarmed to unload the ship. They refused to allow the crew to touch a piece of freight or handle a piece of baggage.

The only difficulty Norman found was to systematize their work under the captain's direction.

The day following they "swarmed" again to clear the lawn of weeds and restore the labyrinth of walks and beds of flowers in the great court. Merchants exchanged the yardstick for the rake and hoe. Preachers laid aside their sermons to wield a spade, and returned from their tasks in the evening with song and laughter.

Among the women the spirit of sacrifice and enthusiastic service was even higher. Many who loved flowers begged the privilege of using the pruning-knife and some even seized a hoe and worked with unwearied zeal.

Others, who had never seen the inside of their own kitchens, rolled up their sleeves, donned white aprons, entered the great cooking-room of the hotel, and made pots and kettles fly. Beautiful girls who had spent lives of comparative ease took turns in waiting on the tables, and all worked with a spirit of joy which robbed labour of its weariness.

By common consent Norman had assumed the general directorship of the colony, and by common consent the Wolfs were accepted as his chief advisers. This arrangement was formally voted on and unanimously approved at the first night's assembly of the Brotherhood in the big dining-hall of the building, which they now christened the "Mission House of the Brotherhood of Man."

On accepting the position of general manager of the Brotherhood the young leader rose and faced the people with deep emotion.

"Comrades," he began, in trembling tones, "I thank you for the confidence you have shown in me. I shall strive to prove myself worthy of your faith, and I hope within a year that we shall make such progress in the development of our new social system that I shall be able to convey then the full title to this glorious island to your permanent organization."

A round of applause greeted this announcement.

"I 'm sure our preliminary work will be completed within a single year. I am not a man of many words, but I hope to prove myself a man of deeds. I shall consult you in every important step to be taken, and for this purpose the General Assembly of the Brotherhood will be held in this hall every Friday evening. On Monday evening a ball will be given for the pleasure of our young people, and every Wednesday evening a social reception. Let us make these three evenings the source of inspiration for our daily tasks."

Norman closed his brief speech in a burst of genuine enthusiasm. Scores of young men and women crowded to the platform and grasped his hand.

When the last echoes of the evening's celebration had died away, Catherine led Barbara into her room.

Wolf sat quietly smoking by the window.

"What on earth 's the matter?" the girl asked. "You drag me to your room half dressed, in the dead of night, and speak in whispers. I thought we 'd done with the dark and scheming ways of the world."

"And so we have, my child," laughed Wolf.

His cold gray eyes lighted with sudden warmth as they rested on Barbara's dainty little figure. Its exquisite lines could be plainly see through the silk kimono as she walked with languid grace and threw the mass of dishevelled curls back from her shoulders.

"Sit down, dear," Catherine said, with a smile. "We have something of the utmost importance to say to you."

"I am to go abroad as an ambassador to some foreign court. Don't say that — I like it here."

"No. We are going to propose that you establish a court here," Wolf interrupted.

"Establish a court!" Barbara exclaimed. "How romantic!"

"In short, my child, it's absolutely necessary for you to become, not merely the power behind the throne with our young Comrade Chief, you must assume the throne itself."

"But how?" the girl asked.

"As if you did n't know!"

"I honestly don't. My eloquence is of little use here. We are all persuaded. Besides, our Comrade Chief has acquired the habit of thinking for himself."

"Just so," observed Wolf. "And we want you to do his thinking for him."

"What do you mean, Catherine?" Barbara

asked, her brow suddenly clouding, as she looked straight into her foster-mother's eyes.

"That you must win young Worth."

"Deliberately set out to make him love me?" the girl exclaimed with scorn. "I 'll do nothing of the kind."

"You must, my dear," Wolf pleaded earnestly. "It 's all for the Cause. It 's in this boy's power to make or wreck this great enterprise. We have a kingdom here whose wealth and power may become the wonder of the world. It may be wrecked by the whim of one man. A thousand difficulties must be faced before we can have smooth sailing. The one thing above all to be done is to secure from young Worth the deed to this island. He must be convinced of the success of the scheme, and he must be convinced before he faces some of the most serious problems that are sure to arise — problems which will demand a strong arm and a cool, clear head to handle. The boy means well, but he can never meet these issues. Win his love and everything will be easy. Slowly and patiently I will perfect the organization we must have to succeed."

"I fail to see the necessity of such a shameless act on my part. No man here is so enthusiastic as our young leader. He is sure to make the deed. You heard his promise to-night."

"He intends to do it, I grant," Catherine argued. "But what Herman and I clearly see is that he will sooner or later be overwhelmed with difficulties. He may quit in disgust at the very moment when a strong policy could save the Cause. We want to be sure. He is a new convert. His enthusiasm is now at white heat. We are afraid of what may happen when it cools."

"With your great brown eyes looking into his," Wolf broke in, "and your little hand in his, it can't cool!"

"I don't think he cares for me in that way at all," the girl protested. "He has held himself quite aloof from me of late."

"All the more reason why your woman's pride should be piqued to make the conquest," urged Wolf.

"I have no such vulgar ambitions," was the short answer.

"Of course you have n't, child," Wolf said in serious tones. "We understand that. But we ask this of you as a brave little soldier of the Cause. It 's the one big, brave thing you can do."

"I might have to let him kiss me," she said, with a frown.

"Well, he 's a handsome youngster — it would n't poison you," laughed Catherine.

"I hate it! I think I hate every man on earth sometimes," she answered.

Wolf laughed and looked at her with quiet intensity.

"Come, dear, you can do this for the Cause we both love," Catherine urged.

"I might have to let him put his arm around me——."

Catherine seized her hand, looked at her steadily for a moment, and slowly said:

"The woman who would not give both her body and her soul for the Cause of Humanity, if called on to make the sacrifice, is not worthy to live in the big world of which we 've dreamed."

Barbara's face flushed and her eyes sparkled.

"You believe this?" she asked, sternly.

"With all my soul," was the fierce answer.

Barbara hesitated a moment, and firmly said: "Then I 'll do it!"

CHAPTER XVI

BARBARA CHOOSES A PROFESSION

WHEN Norman came down to the office next morning, the clerk handed him a note. A glance at the smooth, perfect handwriting told him at once it was from Barbara. He opened it with a smile of pleasant surprise and read with increasing astonishment:

"You are to take breakfast with me this morning in the rose bower of the floral court.

"By order of

"BARBARA BOZENTA,

"*Secretary to the General Manager.*"

Norman found her alone, seated beside a little table in the bower, her face wreathed in mischievous smiles.

She rose and extended her hand:

"Permit me to introduce you to your new secretary."

"I assure you my delight is only equalled by my surprise," he answered, with boyish banter.

"Yes, I thought it best to take you by surprise. Now that it's all settled, I trust we will get on well." She looked at him with demure and charming impudence.

Norman burst into laughter.

"I'm sure we will!" he answered. "All I require is industry, patience, wisdom, tact, knowledge, sacrifice, absolute obedience, and a joyous desire to assume full responsibility for my mistakes!"

"All of which will come to me," she responded, with mock gravity. "Permit me!"

She led him to the chair she had placed beside the table, and poured a cup of coffee for him.

Norman watched her with keen enjoyment. "I've never seen you in this mood before," he said, quietly.

"You like it?"

"Beyond words! I'm afraid I'll wake up directly and find I'm dreaming. I'm sure now, when I look into your eyes, sparkling with fun, that you are a flower nymph, and that your home has always been a rose bower on the sunny slope of a southern hillside."

"Perhaps I'm just teasing you. Perhaps I won't work," she said, glancing at him from the corners of her brown eyes.

"Then you'll find it a serious joke," he answered, firmly. "Resignations are not in order. You have chosen your profession. As general manager I have given my approval. That settles it, does n't it?"

"If you are pleased, yes," she answered, gravely.

"I am more than pleased. I 've been afraid to ask you to do this work for me — though I 've had it in mind."

"Why afraid?"

"I don't know. I somehow got the impression lately that you did n't like me personally."

"How could you think such a thing!" she protested.

"Just a vague impression — caught, perhaps, from little gestures you sometimes made, little frowns that sometimes came to your brow, little flashes of hostility from your eyes."

"I did n't mean it, comrade!" she said, demurely, while her eyes danced and her mouth twitched playfully.

"And you 've fully weighed the cost?"

"Fully."

"You know that you will be forced to spend most of your time in my office?"

"I 'll try to endure it," she laughed.

"Without a frown or a hostile look?"

"Unless you provoke it."

Norman ate in silence for five minutes, listening to Barbara's girlish chatter while she bubbled over with the spirit of pure joy. Her whole being radiated fun and laughter as the sun pours forth heat and light. He wondered where this magic secret of joyous womanhood had been hidden in the past.

"What a revelation you 've been to me this morning," he said, musingly, as he rose from the table.

"How?" she asked.

"I thought you were all seriousness and tragedy, eloquence and pathos."

"We 're in paradise now. The shadows have lifted."

"And I find you a little ray of dancing sunlight."

"So every girl would be if she had the chance."

"And we 're going to give them the chance here, little comrade!" he cried, with enthusiasm.

"I 'll help you!" she earnestly responded, extending her hand with a tender look into the depth of Norman's soul.

CHAPTER XVII

A CALL FOR HEROES

THE first business before the Assembly of the Brotherhood was the permanent assignment of work. The enthusiasm which swept the Socialists through the first week of joyous life could not last. No one expected it. The novelty of their surroundings, the surprise and elation of every one over the beauty and richness of their newly acquired empire, carried the pioneers over the opening days as in a dream. It all seemed like a great picnic — like the long-hoped-for holidays in life of which they had dreamed and never realized, yet which somehow had come to pass.

But the time was at hand to face the first big, sober reality of the new social system. The dining-hall was packed. Every member of the Brotherhood was present.

The orchestra played a lively air in a vain effort to revive the spirit of festivity with which every meeting had hitherto buzzed.

But an evil spirit had entered the Garden of Eden, and joy had fled. Over every heart hovered a brood of solemn questions. What will be my lot? Will I be allowed to choose my work? Or will they tell me what to do? Will it be dirty and disagreeable, or pleasant and inspiring?

Norman sat in his chair of state as presiding officer, bending over a mass of papers which Barbara had spread before him. She leaned close, and a stray hair from one of her brown curls touched his forehead. He trembled and stared blankly at the papers, seeing only a beautiful face.

"You understand?" she asked. "I 've placed under each department the number of workers needed."

"Yes, yes, I understand!" he repeated, looking at her, blankly.

"I don't believe you 've heard a word I 've spoken to you," she said, reproachfully.

He was about to answer when the music stopped. Norman lifted his head with a start, rose quickly and faced the crowd.

"Comrades," be began, "the time has come for us to make good our faith in one another. You have proven yourselves brave and faithful in our struggle with the infamies of the system of capitalism. We call now for the heroes and heroines of actual work. We are entering, under the most favourable auspices, on the most important experiment yet made in the social history of the world. We are going to prove that mankind is one vast brotherhood — that love, not greed, can rule this earth.

"In our temporary organization we wish to outline the forms on which we will later found the permament State of Ventura. At present we will organize four departments — Production, Distribution, Domestic Service, and Education.

"I am going to ask each one of you, by secret ballot, to choose your permanent work."

A cheer shook the building.

Norman flushed with pleasure, and continued quickly:

"It shall be my constant aim as your general manager under our temporary organization to give you the widest personal liberty consistent with the success of our enterprise.

"Before preparing your ballots for choice of your work, I shall have to ask that each head of a family and each unmarried man and woman first pass by the platform and draw lots for the assignment of your rooms in our Mission House. There have been some complaints already, I'm sorry to say, on this question. Some wish to live on the first floor, some on the top, but everybody wants to live on the south side of the house with the glorious views of the sea, and nobody wishes to live on the north side. There is but one way to determine such a question in our ideal state. Fate must decide.

"The numbers of each room and suite are in the basket. The bachelors will be assigned to the right wing, the girls to the left wing, the married ones to the centre of the building.

"Please form in line on the left and march toward the right aisle past the platform."

"Mr. Chairman!" called Roland Adair, the Bard of Ramcat.

Norman rapped for silence, and those who had risen resumed their seats.

"I protest, Mr. Chairman," continued the poet, "against the cruelty of such a process. The weak and the aged should be given their choice first."

"We left them all behind us!" Norman cried, with a wave of his hand. "There are no weak and aged in this crowd. We belong to the elect. We have found the secret of eternal youth."

Another cheer swept the crowd, the poet subsided with a sigh of contempt, and the people quickly filed past the platform and drew their lots for permanent rooms in the building. The larger suites had been subdivided, so that the entire pioneer colony of two thousand found accommodations under one roof.

When the crowd had resumed their seats, and the last cry of triumph over a successful draw and the last groan of disappointment over an unlucky lot had subsided, Norman rose and made the most momentous announcement the Brotherhood had yet heard:

"In the Department of Production we need hod-carriers, bricklayers, carpenters, architects, teamsters, and skilled mechanics for the foundry and machine-shops, saw-mill, and flour mills. On the farm and orchard we need ploughmen and harvesters for grain and hay, gardeners, stablemen, and ditchers.

"In our Department of Domestic Service we need cooks, seamstresses, washerwomen, scrubbers and cleaners, waiters, porters, bell-boys, telephone girls, steamfitters, plumbers, chimney-sweeps, and sewer cleaners.

"In the Department of Education we need artists and artisans, teachers, nurses, printers and binders, pressmen and compositors, one editor, scientists and lecturers, missionaries, actors, singers, and authors.

"Now you each of you know what you can do best. Choose the work in which you can render your comrades the highest service of which you are capable and best advance the cause of humanity. Write your name and your choice of work on the blanks which have been furnished you."

The orchestra played while the ballots were being cast and counted.

The chairman at length rose with the tabulated sheet in his hand and faced his audience.

"Comrades," he said, with a twinkle in his eye, "that old saying I 'll have to repeat, 'If at first you don't succeed, try, try again!' Beyond the shadow of a doubt we shall have to try this election again. If I did n't know by the serious look on your faces that you mean it I 'd say off-hand that you were trying to put up a joke on me."

He paused, and a painful silence followed.

"Give us the ballot!" growled the Bard.

Norman looked at the list he held, and in spite of himself, as he caught the gleam of mischief in Barbara's eye, burst into laughter and sat down.

Wolf ascended the platform, glanced over the list and whispered:

"It 's a waste of time. Call for the election of an executive council with full powers."

"We 'll try once more," Norman insisted, quickly rising.

"Comrades, I 'm sorry to say there is no election. We must proceed to another ballot, and if the industries absolutely necessary to the existence of any society are not voted into operation, we must then choose an executive council with full power to act. I appeal to your sense of heroism and self-sacrifice ——"

"Give us the ballot! Read it!" thundered the offended poet.

"Yes, read it!"

"Read it!"

The shouts came from all parts of the hall. The crowd was in dead earnest and could n't see the joke.

Once more the young chairman raised the fateful record of human frailty before his eyes, paused, and then solemnly began:

"In the first place, comrades, more than six hundred ballots out of the two thousand cast are invalid. They have been cast for work not asked for. They must be thrown out at once.

"Three hundred and sixty five able-bodied men choose hunting as their occupation. I grant you that game is plentiful on the island, but we can't spare you, gentlemen!

"Two hundred and thirty-five men want to fish! The waters abound in fish, but we have a pound-net which supplies us with all we can eat.

"Thirty-two men and forty-six women wish to preach.

"We do not need at present hunters, fishermen, or preachers, and have not called for volunteers in these departments of labour.

"Three hundred and fifty-six women wish to go on the stage, and one hundred and ninety-five of them choose musical comedy and light opera. I think this includes most of our female population between the ages of fourteen and thirty-five!"

A murmur of excitement swept the feminine portion of the audience.

"Allow me to say," he went on, "that the most urgent need of the colony at this moment cannot be met by organizing a chorus, however beautiful and pleasing its performances would be. We need, and we must have, waitresses and milkmaids. The chorus can wait, the cows cannot.

"I asked for one editor. One hundred and seventy-five men and sixty-three women have chosen that field. Seventy-five men and thirty-two women wish to be musicians."

"We have looked in vain among the ballots for a single hod-carrier, or ploughman, ditcher, cook, seamstress, washerman or washerwoman, stableman, scrubber, or cleaner. The Brotherhood cannot live a day without them. Remember, comrades, we are to make the great experiment on which the future happiness of the race may depend. Let us forget our selfish preferences and think only of our fellow men. I call for heroes of the hod, heroines of the washtub and the scrubbing-brush and milk-pail, knights of the pitchfork, spade, and shovel. Let hunters, fishermen, preachers, and chorus-girls forget they live for the present.

"This is not a joke, comrades, though I have laughed. It's one of the gravest problems we must face. It has been suggested that we hire outside labour to do this disagreeable work for a generation or two. The moment we dare make such a compromise we are lost forever. We must solve this problem or quit. A second ballot is ordered at once."

Again the orchestra played, the ushers passed the boxes, the vote was taken, and all for naught. Not a single hero of the hod appeared. Not a single heroine of the washtub, the scrubbing-brush, or the milk-pail.

The young chairman's face was very grave when Barbara handed him the results.

She bent and whispered:

"Away with frowns and doubts and fears! There's a better way. A leader must lead. Their business is to follow."

Norman's face brightened. He turned to the crowd, and in tones of clear, ringing command announced:

"Comrades, I had hoped you could choose your work of your own accord. The attempt has failed. Six divisions of labour, each of them absolutely essential to the existence of society in any form above the primitive savage, have not a single man or woman in them."

"We must elect an executive council of four who shall sit as a court of last resort in settling the question of the ability of each comrade and the work to which he shall be assigned. Under our temporary charter the general manager will preside over this court and cast the deciding vote. Nominations are in order for the other four. We want two men and two women in this council. In all our deliberations woman shall have equal voice with man.

The Bard made a speech of protest against the action about to be taken, in the sacred name of liberty.

"This act is the first step on the road to a tyranny more monstrous than any ever devised by capitalism!" he shouted, with hands uplifted, his long hair flying in wild disorder.

Tom Mooney, an old miner, who had met Norman and become his friend during a visit to one of his father's mines, sprang to his feet and made a rush for the excited poet. Confronting him a moment, Tom inquired:

"Kin I ax ye a few questions?"

"Certainly. As many as you like."

"Kin ye cook?"

"I cannot."

"Kin ye wash?"

"No!"

"Kin ye scrub?"

"No, sir."

"Ever swing a hod?"

"I have not."

"Ever milk a cow?"

"No!"

"Are ye willin' to learn them things?"

"I did n't come here for that purpose."

"Then, what t' 'ell ye kickin' about?" Tom cried, and, glaring at the poet, he thundered fiercely:

"Set down!"

The man of song was so disconcerted by this unexpected onslaught, and by the roars of laughter which greeted Tom's final order, that he dropped into his seat, muttering incoherent protests, and the balloting for the executive council proceeded at once amid universal good humour.

A dozen names were proposed as candidates, and the four receiving the highest votes were declared duly elected.

The election resulted in the choice of Herman Wolf, Catherine, Barbara Bozenta, and Thomas Mooney.

Tom was amazed at his sudden promotion to

high office, and insisted on resigning in favour of a man of better education.

Norman caught his big horny hand and pressed it.

"Not on your life, Tom. You've made a hit. The people like your hard horse-sense. You will make a good judge. Besides, I need you. You're a man I can depend on every day in the year."

"I'll stick ef you need me, boy — but I hain't fitten, I tell ye."

"I'll vouch for your fitness — sit down!"

The last command Norman thundered into Tom's ears in imitation of his order to the poet, and the old miner, with a grin, dropped into his seat.

As Norman was about to declare the meeting adjourned, the steward ascended the platform and whispered a message.

The young leader turned to the crowd and lifted his hand for silence.

"Comrades, a prosaic but very important announcement I have to make. I have just been informed that there is no milk for supper. The cows have been neglected. They must be milked. I call for a dozen volunteer milkmaids until this adjustment can be made. Come, now! — and a dozen young men to assist them. Let's make this a test of your loyalty to the cause. All labour is equally honourable. Labour is the service of your fellow man. Who will be the first heroine to fill this breach in the walls of our defence?"

Barbara sprang forward, with uplifted head, laughing.

"I will!"

"And I'll help you!" Norman cried, with a laugh. "Who will join us now? Come, you pretty chorus-girls! You would n't mind if you carried these milk-pails on the stage in a play. Well, this is the biggest stage you will ever appear on, and all the millions of the civilized world are watching."

A pretty, rosy-cheeked girl joined Barbara.

An admirer followed, and in a moment a dozen girls and their escorts had volunteered. They formed in line and marched to the cow lot with Norman and Barbara leading, singing and laughing and swinging their milk-pails like a crowd of rollicking children.

When they reached the pasture where the cows were herded, Norman asked Barbara, with some misgivings:

"Honestly, did you ever milk a cow?"

"Of course I have," she promptly replied. "I spent two years on a farm once. Do you think

I'd make a fool of myself trying before all these kids if I had n't?"

"I did n't know but that you made a bluff at it to lead the others on. What can I do, for heaven's sake?"

Norman looked at her in a helpless sort of way while Barbara rolled up her sleeves. For the first time he saw her beautifully rounded bare arm to its full length. He stood with open-eyed admiration. Never had he seen anything so white and round and soft, so subtly and seductively suggestive of tenderness and love.

"For heaven's sake, what do I do?" he repeated, blankly.

"Get some meal in that bucket for my cow, and see that her calf don't get to her — I'll do the rest."

Norman hustled to the barn with the other boys, got his bucket of meal, placed it in front of the cow Barbara had selected, and stood watching with admiration the skill with which her deft little hands pressed two streams of white milk into the bucket at her feet.

"Goodness, you 're a wonder," he cried, admiringly. "But where 's the calf I 'm supposed to be watching?"

"I think that 's the one standing close to the gate in the next lot watching me with envy. The first time the gate 's opened he 'll jump through if he gets half a chance — so look out!"

"I 'll watch him," Norman promised, without lifting his eyes from the rhythmic movement of the bare white arms.

He had scarcely spoken when a careless boy swung the gate wide open, and the lusty calf, whose soft eyes had been watching Barbara through the fence, made a break for his mother. In a swift, silent rush he planted one foot in Barbara's milk-pail, knocked her over with the other, switched his tail, and fell to work on his own account without further concern. It was all done so suddenly it took Norman's breath. He sprang to Barbara's side and helped her to her feet.

Norman grabbed the calf by the ear with one hand and by the tail with the other, and started toward the gate.

The animal suddenly ducked his head, plunged forward, jerked Norman to his knees, and dragged him ten yards before he could regain his feet. The young leader rose, tightened his grip, and started with a rush toward the gate, but the calf swerved in time to avoid it, gaining speed with each step, and started off with his escort in a mad race around the lot, galloping at a terrific speed, bellowing and snorting at every jump.

The others stopped their work to laugh and cheer as round and round the maddened little brute flew with the tall, heroic leader galloping by his side.

Norman had no time to call for help. He could n't let go and he could n't stop the calf.

As he made the second round of the lot, upsetting buckets, smashing milk-pails, and stampeding peaceful cows, a boy yelled through the roars of laughter:

"Twist his tail! Twist his tail an' he 'll go the way you want him!"

Norman misunderstood the order, loosened the head and grabbed the tail with both hands. With a loud bellow the calf plunged into a wilder race around the lot, dragging his tormentor now with regular, graceful easy jumps. He made the rounds twice thus, single file, amid screams of laughter, suddenly turned and plunged headlong through an osage hedge, and left Norman sitting in a dusty heap on the ground among the thorns. He rose, brushed his clothes sheepishly, and looked through the hedge at the calf which had turned and stood eyeing him now with an expression of injured innocence.

Barbara came up, wiping the tears of laughter from her eyes.

"I 've learned something new," Norman quietly

observed. "All labour may be equally honourable. It's not equally expedient. I wish you'd look at that beast eyeing me through the fence! It's positively uncanny. I believe he's possessed of the devil. I don't wonder at that belief of the ancients. I've tackled many a brute on the football field — but this is one on me!"

The brilliant young leader of the new moral world led the procession of milkmaids back to the house as the shadows of evening fell, a sadder but wiser man for the day's experience.

CHAPTER XVIII

A NEW ARISTOCRACY

THREE members of the executive council, Norman, Barbara, and Tom, began at once the task of assigning work. The problems which immediately faced the council were overwhelming, but they were urgent and could admit of no delay. The absolute refusal of every member of the Brotherhood to do the dirty and disagreeable work brought at once two issues to a crisis. Either labour must be voluntary or involuntary. The people who did this work must be induced to agree to perform it or they must be forced to do it by a superior authority without their consent.

They could only be led to choose this work by inducements of an extraordinary nature — the payment of enormously high wages and the shortening of each day's work to a ridiculous minimum.

If wages were made unequal, the old problem of inequality would remain unsolved. For equal wages no man would lift his hand.

Confronted by this dilemma the executive

council decided at once to fix wages on an unequal basis rather than reduce its unwilling members to a condition of involuntary labour, which is merely a long way to spell slavery.

When this decision was announced, Roland Adair, the Bard of Ramcat, once more lifted his voice in solemn protest:

"I denounce this act in the name of every principle which has brought us together," he cried, with solemn warning. "You have established a system far more infamous than the unequal wages of the old society where the law of the survival of the fittest is the court of last resort. You have opened the door of fathomless corruption by substituting the whim of an executive council for the law of nature. It is the beginning of jealousy, strife, favouritism, jobbery, and injustice."

"Then what's a better way?" Old Tom asked, with a sneer.

"It's your business to find a better way," cried the man of visions.

Tom glared at the poet with a look of fury and Norman whispered to the old miner:

"Remember, Tom, you're sitting as a judge in the Supreme Court of State!"

"Can't help it. I never did have no use for a fool. Ef he can't tell us a better way, let 'im shet up."

Barbara pressed Tom's arm, and he subsided.

The court at once entered into the question of wages for domestic service.

It had been agreed, at the suggestion of the Wolfs, that they should spend their time in quietly investigating the qualifications of each member of the Brotherhood for the work to be assigned, and make their reports in secret to the majority of the court, which should sit continuously until all had been decided.

Neither Norman, Barbara, nor the old miner suspected for a moment the deeper motive which Wolf concealed behind this withdrawal from the decision of these cases. They found out in a very startling way later.

The chief cook demanded a hundred dollars a month.

Old Tom snorted with contempt. Norman smiled and spoke kindly:

"Remember, Louis, you only received $75 a month in San Francisco. Here the Brotherhood provides every man with his food, his clothes, and his house. Wages are merely the inducement used to satisfy each individual that labour may still be done by free contract, not by force."

"Well, it 'll take a hundred a month to satisfy me," was the stolid reply. "I did n't come here to cook. I could do that in the old hell we lived in. I came here to do better and bigger things. I can do them, too ——"

"But we 've fixed the salary of the general manager at only seventy-five dollars a month, and you demand a hundred?"

"I do, and if the general manager prefers my job, I 'll trade with you and guarantee to do your work better than it 's being done."

"Yes, you will!" old Tom growled, as he leaned over Barbara and whispered to Norman.

"Make it thirty dollars a month, and if he don't go to work — leave him to me, I 'll beat him till he does it."

"No, we can't manage it that way, Tom. We must try to satisfy him."

"Hit 's a hold-up, I tell ye — highway robbery — the triflin' son of a gun! Don't you say so, miss?" Tom appealed earnestly to Barbara.

"We must have cooks, Tom — and we want everybody to be happy."

"Make him cook, make him — that 's his business — I 'd do it if I knowed how. He 's got to take what we give 'im. He can't git off this island. He enlisted for five years. If he deserts, court-martial and shoot him."

In spite of old Tom's bitter protest, Norman and Barbara succeeded in persuading the chief cook to accept eighty-five dollars a month —

an advance of ten dollars over the highest wages he had ever received before.

When the eighteen assistant cooks lined up for the settlement of their wages a new problem of unexpected proportions was presented. They had listened attentively to the case of the chef, and their chosen orator presented his argument in brief but emphatic words:

"We demand the exact wages you have voted the chef."

"Well, what do ye think er that?" old Tom groaned to Norman. "Hit's jist like I told ye. Hit's a hold-up."

"We must persuade them, Tom," the young leader replied.

"Let me persuade 'em!" the old miner pleaded.

"How?" Barbara asked, with a twinkle in her brown eyes.

"I'll line 'em up agin that wall and trim their hair with my six-shooter. I won't hurt 'em. But when I finish the job I'll guarantee they'll do what I tell 'em without any back talk. You folks take a walk and make me Chief Justice fer an hour, and when you come back we'll have peace and plenty. Jest try it now, and don't you butt in. Let me persuade 'em!"

Norman shook his head.

"Keep still, Tom! We must reason with them."

"Ye 're wastin' yer breath," the miner drawled in disgust.

"Don't you think, comrades," Norman began, in persuasive tones, "that your demands are rather high?"

"Certainly not," was the prompt reply. "We come here to get equal rights. We don't want to cook. I 'm a born actor, myself. I expected to play in Shakespeare when I joined the Brotherhood. Anybody that wants this job can have it. If we do your hot, dirty, disgusting, disagreeable work while the others play in the shade we are going to get something for it."

"Even so," the young leader responded, "is it fair that an assistant cook should receive equal wages with the chef?"

"And why not? Labour creates all value. The chef 's a fakir. We do all the work. He never lifts his hand to a pot or pan. He struts and loafs through the kitchen and lords it over the men. Let him try to run the kitchen without us, and see how much you get to eat! We stand on the equal rights of man!"

"But my dear comrade ——"

"Don't use them words," old Tom pleaded, "jest let me make a few remarks ——"

Barbara pinched Tom's arm and he subsided.

"Can't you see," Norman went on, "that we

are paying the chef for his directive ability, for his inventive genius in creating new dishes and making old ones more delicious? You but execute his orders."

"We stand square on our principles. Labour creates all values. The chef never works. We make every dish that goes to the table. If it has any value we make it. We demand our rights!"

The court agreed on fifty dollars a month, and the men refused to consider it.

"We prefer to work in the fields, the foundry, the machine-shop, the mills, the forests, anywhere you like except the kitchen. Let the chef do your work. Good day!"

They turned and marched out in a body and sat down in the sunshine.

In vain Norman argued and pleaded. They stood their ground with sullen determination.

A final clincher which the young leader could not evade always ended the argument. The spokesman came back to it with dogged persistence:

"What did you mean, then, when you've been drumming into our ears that labour creates all value? We do all the work, don't we?"

The upshot of it was the eighteen assistant cooks marched back into the hall, stood before the judges, and all were granted equal wages with the chef.

Whereupon the chef sprang to his feet and faced the court with blazing eyes.

"You grant these chumps — these idiots — wages equal to mine? Not one of them has brains enough to cook an egg if I did n't tell him how. Their wages equal to mine. I resign!"

Tom spoke vigorously:

"Now will ye leave him to me?"

Norman and Barbara looked at each other in angry and helpless amazement.

The old miner leaped to his feet, made his way down from the platform, and with two swift strides reached the chef. He leaned close and whispered something in the rebel's ear. There was a moment's hesitation and the chef turned, signalled to his assistants, and amid cheers marched to the kitchen.

Tom resumed his seat beside Barbara with a smile, quietly saying:

"That 's the way to do business, ladies and gentlemen!"

"What did you say to him?" Barbara asked.

"Oh, nothin' much," was the careless answer.

"I hope you did n't threaten him, Tom?" Norman asked with some misgiving.

"Na — I did n't threaten him. I spoke quiet and peaceable."

"But what did you tell him?" the young leader persisted.

"I jest told him I'd give him two minutes ter git back ter the kitchen or I'd blow his head off!"

"I'm afraid our table will feel the effects of that remark, Tom," Barbara said, doubtfully.

Next to the question of cooks the most urgent issue to be settled was the case of the scrubbers, cleaners, and drainmen. The women who had been assigned to the tasks of scrubbing the floors, washing the windows and dishes, had watched the triumphs of the cooks with keen appreciation of their own power. It was easy to see that the more disagreeable and disgusting the character of the work, the more extravagant the demands which could be made and enforced. The scrubbers and dishwashers boldy demanded one hundred dollars a month and six hours for a working day, and refused with sullen determination to argue the question.

To Barbara's mild and gentle protest their answer was complete and stunning:

"You have assigned us this dirty job. Do you want it at any price?" asked their orator. "I'll take yours without wages and jump at the chance."

Tom lost all interest in the proceedings and drew himself up in a knot in his chair. Now and then a growl came from the depths of his throat.

Once he was heard to distinctly articulate:
"This makes me tired."

The court begged and pleaded, cajoled, argued in vain with the stubborn scrubwomen. Not an inch would they move in their demands. The floors were becoming unspeakably filthy. They had not been scrubbed since the arrival of the colony.

Norman turned to Barbara.

"Put the question solemnly to ourselves — we don't want the job at any price, do we?"

"I could n't do it!" she admitted, frankly.

"Then what 's the use? We must be fair. It 's worth what they ask."

The court granted the demands and the scrubwomen and dishwashers marched to the kitchen and once more the chef tore his hair and cursed the fate which brought him to such disgrace as to work with stupid subordinates at equal wages and gaze on dishwashers and scrubwomen whose wages exceeded his own.

The climax of all demands was reached when the drainman demanded a hundred and fifty dollars a month and four hours for each working day.

Norman looked at him in dumb confusion. He knew what he was going to say before he opened his mouth and he had no answer.

The drainman bowed low in mock humility but the proud wave of his hand belied his words.

"My calling was a humble one in the old world, Comrade Judges," he said. "I came here to climb mountain heights and find my way among the stars. You have sent me back to the sewers. I always felt that I had missed my true calling. I 've always wanted to be a poet ———"

The Bard shook his mane and groaned.

"I don't want this job at any price. But the sewers are choked. They have not been cleaned for two years. It must be done. I 've named my price. I 'll gladly yield to any man who envies my luck. If such a man is here let him speak — or forever hereafter hold his peace."

With a grandiloquent gesture the drainman swept the crowd with his eye, but no man responded.

The court granted his demand.

The Bard leaped once more to his feet and entered his protest. This time old Tom listened with interest. His concluding sentence rang with bitter irony:

"Against these absurd decisions I lift my voice once more in solemn protest. We came to this charmed island to abolish all class distinctions. You have destroyed the old classes based on culture, achievement, genius, wealth, and power.

You have created a new aristocracy on whose shield is emblazoned — a dish-rag and scrubbing-brush encircled by a sewer pipe! I make my most humble bow to our new king — the drainman! I hail the apotheosis of the scrub-woman!"

"Say, you give me a pain — shut up" thundered Tom.

The singer collasped with a sigh and the crowd laughed.

The foreman of the farm brought two men before the court and asked for important instructions.

"Comrade Judges," he began, "I had two men assigned to me a week ago whom I don't want and won't have at any price. I return them to the Brotherhood with thanks. You can do what you please with them."

"What's the matter?" Norman asked, with some irritation.

The foreman shoved and kicked a man in front of the judges.

"This fool ——"

"You must not use such language, Mr. Fore-man," Barbara interrupted.

"I beg your pardon, Comrade Judges," he apologized. "This coyote I put on a mowing-machine yesterday. He said he knew how to run it. He broke it on a smooth piece of ground the first hour. I gave him another and he wrecked it before noon. It will take the labour of five men two days to repair the damage he has done. I don't want him at any price."

"What have you to say?" Norman asked the accused.

"It wasn't my fault. The thing broke itself."

"But how did it happen twice the same day, sonny?" Tom asked.

"I dunno. Hit jist happened," was the dogged answer.

"I've another scoundrel ——"

"You must not use such language," Barbara broke in.

"Again begging the pardon of Comrade Judges," the foreman continued: "This dog — he kicked another slovenly looking lout before the judges — "tore to pieces the shoulders of two pairs of horses with careless harnessing before I found him and kicked him out of the stables. Those four horses can't work for a month. We'll have to pay at least $500 for two teams right away to take their places, or lose a crop of hay."

Tom glared at the culprit.

"What did ye ruin them horses' shoulders fer?"

"I didn't know it," was the sulking answer.

"He's a liar!" cried the foreman. "He put the same collars on their galled necks three days in succession and beat them unmercifully when they could n't pull the load."

"What do you say, Tom?" Norman asked.

The old miner glared at the last culprit and his grim mouth tightened:

"Wall, you kin do as ye please, but any man that 'll abuse a hoss will commit murder. I'd put the fust one in the cow lot to shovellin' compost. This one I'd quietly lynch — no public rumpus about it — jest take 'im down by the beach, hang 'im to one of them posts on the pier, shoot 'im full of holes, and drop 'im into the sea to be sure he don't come back to life."

Norman conferred with Barbara a moment and rendered the decision:

"Mr. Foreman, the first man is transferred from the field machinery to the compost-heap in the barnyard. The second man who disabled the horses will assist in cleaning the sewers. Their wages will remain the same as before."

A round of applause greeted this decision.

The Bard renewed his attack with unusual zeal. Standing before the court and shaking his long hair he cried:

"At last the climax of tyranny! Two comrades condemned without a jury and without defence! I congratulate you. In one day you have established an aristocracy of filth and created a penal colony without a hearing or appeal. We are making progress."

The old miner grunted, Barbara smiled tenderly at Norman, and the court adjourned.

CHAPTER XIX

SOME TROUBLES IN HEAVEN

NORMAN found it necessary for the executive council to sit continuously for the adjustment of disputes and the settlement of new problems which arose at every step of progress in the new moral world.

He had condemned the sins of the old world of capitalism with cocksure certainty. Now that he had been made a supreme judge with power to adjust the rights and wrongs of his fellow man, he was appalled at the magnitude of the task of substituting an ideal for the reign of natural law under which civilization had been slowly evolved.

There were two men in the Brotherhood whom he grew early to hate with cordial, thorough, murderous hatred — Roland Adair, the Bard of Ramcat, who always denounced every decision as unjust, and a tall, hooked-nosed, stoopshouldered, scholarly looking man named Diggs, who invariably sat near him and at every conceivable opportunity asked questions. These questions were always put in an innocent, friendly way, but when Diggs looked at him through his gleaming spectacles Norman always got the impression that an imp of the devil had suddenly popped up through the floor.

The first day after the general assignment of work Diggs rose before the council, adjusted his glasses, and drew a piece of paper from his pocket. Norman knew before he spoke that the document bristled with questions. Diggs's glasses had always fascinated him, but to-day they seemed of unusual thickness and enormous size, and their concave surfaces seemed to flash light from a thousand angles.

Diggs adjusted them on his hook-nose with deliberation and glanced carefully over his notes before speaking.

Norman turned to Barbara with a sigh.

She pressed his hand in silent sympathy.

"Don't worry!" she whispered.

Norman's breath quickened as he answered the pressure of the soft, warm fingers but he managed to move his chair and break the effects of her spell without revealing to her the effort it cost. Each hour of their association he felt the cords he dare not try to break tighten about his heart. He determined each day to put the thought from him. Over and over again with grim resolution he repeated his vow:

"I'll keep a clear head. I've got to decide this issue on its merits. I owe it to my generous friends who made it possible."

He had avoided her for the last few days. She guessed the cause intuitively and knew that he was fighting with desperation to escape the net she was slowly weaving about him. She began to watch the struggle now with a curious fascination in which cruelty and tenderness were equally mixed. The idea of surrendering her own heart had never once entered her pretty head.

Her life had been lived in a strange war with human society. Man had always appeared to her imagination as an enemy. She had never trusted one — least of all Wolf, the big, impassive animal who had dominated the life of her foster-mother.

With deliberate and cruel art she had set out to master the heart of the man who sat by her side. The task was accepted as part of her work. She had enlisted as a soldier in the Cause. She had received the orders from headquarters. When the deed was done she would turn to a greater task. She had expected to be bored by his idiotic love making. Now her curiosity was beginning to be piqued by his silence. She began vaguely to wonder each moment what kind of pictures she was making in his mind. Her brown eyes searched the depths of his soul in a dumb way that sent the blood rushing to Norman's heart, but each time he had eluded her.

He sat in moody silence now, giving no response to her words of cheer. She roused him from his reverie with a plaintive protest.

"What's the matter? Have I, too, offended?"

He turned quickly and crushed her hand in his strong grasp:

"For heaven's sake don't *you* get into the habit of asking me questions! How could you offend? Your face is my lighthouse set on the cliffs, calm, serene, joyful. I could n't get through a day without you."

A smiling answer was just trembling on her lips when Diggs began to speak.

"Now for the human interrogation point," Barbara laughed.

"Comrade Judges," Diggs began, with guileless good humour, "while we are shaping the form of our ideal State for its permanent organization I wish to submit some questions which may help us in our search for truth."

"Questions," Norman whispered, "which any fool can ask, but the angels of God can't answer."

"But we will answer them!" she flashed, with defiant courage.

"We agree," Diggs went on, "that society must be governed in some way. There must be rulers, but how shall we choose our rulers, and with what powers shall we clothe them? We can begin to see that the head of our social system must at times exercise the full powers of the State. Into whose hands can this enormous power be entrusted, and how shall he be called to account?"

Diggs paused, and Norman flushed at this question, for he took it as a personal thrust. He had occasion to change his mind later.

"How can we," the questioner went on, "retain our democratic liberties as law makers as we grow in numbers? Now we can all meet in general assembly. When the State numbers even five thousand this will not be possible. Will not our politics become even more corrupt than the old system, seeing how enormous the power over the smallest details of life which these legislators possess?

"As our society grows — and thousands are now clamouring for admission — how is wealth to be distributed? Who shall determine, in this larger society, who shall be common labourers, who poets, artists, musicians, preachers, managers? Who shall appoint editors? And who shall call them to account if they publish treason against the State? What shall be done with the ever-increasing number of the lazy, dishonest, and criminal members of the community?

"Who shall determine how much mental work is equivalent to so much manual labour, seeing how vast is the difference in the value of one man's brain product over another's? How can men who are not artists, poets, or musicians determine the value of such work? Or how can one poet be just to his rival if he be made the judge? When our theatre is opened, who shall select the actors? Who shall decide whether they are incompetent? Who shall decide on the selection of the star? What shall be done with an actor, for example, who should spit in the face of a judge deciding adversely? Suppose a man offends the judge? Shall he be punished? If so, who shall do it?

"How can we prevent a man from losing his wages playing poker with his neighbour if he does so joyfully?

"What shall be done with a man who works outside regular hours and accumulates a vast private fortune?"

"Say, ain't you worked your jaw overtime now?" old Tom broke in rudely. "We'll take them things up when we come to 'em. We got somethin' else to do now — set down!"

"These are only friendly suggestions for thought

as we develop our ideal," Diggs answered, with smiling good nature, as he resumed his seat.

"What makes me want to kill that man," Norman muttered to Barbara," is the unfailing politeness and unction with which he asks those questions."

"Patience! patience!" was the low, musical reply. "These little things will all adjust themselves."

Methodist John pressed to the front and poured out to the judges a story of wrong and asked for justice.

"Miss Barbara," he began, in plaintive tones, "you was always good to me in the other world, but since we 've got here even you don't seem the same. Everybody 's hard and cold. They hain't got no sympathy here for a poor man. In the other world I missed my callin' — I was born for the ministry. I come here to serve the Lord. And now they make me work so hard I ain't even got time to pray. I ask for a licence to preach the gospel. Just give me a chance. They 've put me to feedin' hogs and tendin' ter calves. I ain't fit for such work. I want to call sinners to repentance, not swine to their swill. I tell ye I 've been buncoed. It ain't a square deal. I left the poorhouse to come with you to heaven and, by gum, I 've landed in the workhouse——"

"And ef yer don't shet up and git back ter yer work," Tom thundered, "you 'll land in the hospital — you hear me!"

"I ain't er talkin' to you, you cussin, swearin', ungodly son of the devil," the old man answered.

"Come, come, John," Norman interrupted, as he held Tom back. "We can't grant your request. We are not ready to undertake religious work yet."

"Well, God knows ye need it!" John muttered, as the crowd pushed him away.

At the door Catherine greeted him as he passed out, whispered encouraging words, and sent him back to his tasks more cheerful. She had taken her stand thus each day; and, while Wolf was busy quietly mingling with the men outside getting the facts as to the progress of each department, the tall graceful woman of soft voice and madonna face was fast becoming the friend and sympathizer of each discontented worker. She had now assumed the task of peacemaker after each harsh decision had been rendered, and did her work with rare skill — a skill which promised big results in the dawning State of Ventura.

Uncle Bob Worth, an old Negro, bowed low before the judges. He had been a slave of Norman's grandfather in North Carolina and had joined the colony out of admiration for the young leader.

"Marse Norman," he solemnly began.

"Don't call me 'master,' Bob," Norman inter-rupted. "Remember that we are all comrades here."

"Yassah! Yassah! Marse Norman, I try to 'member dat sah, but 'pears ter me dey 's somefin' wrong bout dis whole 'comrade' business, sah! I 'se er 'comrade' now but I 'se wuss off dan I eber wuz. 'Fo' I come here I wuz er butler, and I wuz er gemmen—yas-sah, ef I do hat ter say it myself—and I allus live wid gemmens an' sociate wid gemmens. I come out here wid you ter be a white man an' er equal. Dat 's what dey all say. I be er equal 'comrade.' I make up my mind dat I jine de minstrel band, pick de banjer, an' sing de balance er my life. Bress God, what happen. Dey make me a hod-carrier and make me 'sociate wid low-down po' white trash. I ain't come here ter be no 'comrade' wid dem kin' er folks. Dey ain't my equal, sah, an' I can't 'ford to 'sociate wid 'em. What 's fuddermo, sah, carryin' a hod ain't my business—hit don't suit my health an' brick-dust ain't good fur my com-plexion, sah!"

Tom grunted contemptuously.

Norman smiled and shook his head.

"Sorry, Comrade Bob," he replied. "We haven't men enough to organize the minstrels yet.

We must rush the new building. We have thousands of new members clamouring to join We have nowhere to house them."

"Yassah, an' I 'spec' dey 'll be clamourin' ter unjine fo' long," old Bob muttered, as he passed on to be comforted by Catherine's soothing words.

Saka, the Indian, whom Colonel Worth had educated, had followed Norman. He demanded a return ticket to the Colonel's hunting lodge.

It was promptly refused. Catherine attempted to soothe his ruffled feelings. He snapped his fingers in her face and grunted.

The Brotherhood of Man saw Saka no more for many moons, but the crack of his rifle was heard on the mountain side and the smoke of his tepee curled defiantly from the neighbouring plains.

The chef appeared before the court in answer to numerous complaints about the table.

"I must have the law laid down for the tables, Comrade Judges," he demanded. "One man wants one thing and another refuses to eat at the table where such food is served. A dozen men and women ask only for bread, vegetables, and nuts. They refuse to eat meat. They refuse to allow me to cook it or any one else to eat it if they can help it. They make my life miserable. I want permission to kick them out of the kitchen. They demand the right to inspect my pots and pans to see if meat has touched them. They must go or I go. I will not be insulted by fools. If you do not give me permission to kick these people out of the kitchen I will do so without permission. You can take your choice."

The cook mopped his brow and sat down with a defiant wave of his arm.

A woman who had been a leader of the W. C. T. U. pressed forward before the cook's demand could be considered.

"And I demand in the name of truth, purity, righteousness, justice, faith, and God, that no more wine be allowed on the table. I demand that we burn the wine house and issue an order to the cook never again, under penalty of imprisonment for life, to use a drop of alcohol in the food he serves to the Brotherhood ——"

"And I also demand, Comrade Judges," the cook interrupted, "the right to throw that woman out of the kitchen and have her fined and imprisoned the next time she dares to interfere with my business. She got into the pantry yesterday and destroyed five hundred mince pies because she smelled brandy in them."

"Yes, and I'll do it again if you dare to poison the bodies and souls of my comrades with that hellish stuff!" she cried, triumphantly.

"I'd like to know," the cook shouted, "how I'm to do my work if every fool in creation can butt into my business?"

"Softly! Softly!" Norman warned.

"I mean it!" thundered the chef. "This woman swears she will wreck the dining-room if I dare to place wine again on our bill of fare. I want to know if she's in command of this colony? If so, you can count me out!"

"And while we are on this point, Comrade Judges," spoke up a mild-looking little man, "I have summoned a neighbour of mine to appear before you and show cause why he should *not* cease to have sauerkraut served at breakfast. He sits at my table. I've begged him to stop it. I've begged the cook to stop cooking the stuff, but he bribes the cook ——"

"That's a lie," shouted the chef.

"I saw him do it, your honours," the little man went on. "I'm a small-sized man or I'd lick him. I tried to move my seat but they wouldn't let me. I pledge you my word when he brings that big dish of steaming sauerkraut to our table it fogs the whole end of the dining-room. The odour is so strong it not only stops you from eating, you can't think. It knocks you out for the day."

"Is it possible," Norman inquired, "that there

is a human being among us who eats sauerkraut for breakfast?"

"There's no doubt about it, comrade," promptly responded a tall, strapping-looking fellow, with a dark, scholarly face, as he stepped to the front.

"That's him!" cried the little accuser. "I made him come. Told him I'd organize a party to lynch him if he did n't. He won't dare deny it. I can prove it."

"I have no desire to deny that I eat sauerkraut, you little ape," he replied with scorn. "I come of German ancestry, comrades. My great-grandfather helped to create this nation. He was a pure-blooded German. I inherit from him my personal likes and dislikes. Sauerkraut is the best breakfast food ever served to man. It is a pure vegetable malt. It is wholesome, clean, healthful, and keeps the system of a brain worker in perfect order. I eat it with ham gravy and good hot wheat biscuits. It is some trouble for the cook to prepare this particular kind of soft tea-biscuit for me. I paid him a little extra for this bread — not the kraut. I suggest to your honours that you make sauerkraut a standard breakfast diet as a health measure. They may kick a little at first, but I assure you it will improve the health and character of the colony. If this little chap who

accuses me were put on a diet of kraut for breakfast it might even now make a man of him. I
not only have nothing to apologize for, I bring
you good tidings. I proclaim sauerkraut the
onlyperfect health food for breakfast, and I suggest
its compulsory use. The man who sits next to me
eats snails. I think the habit a filthy and dangerous one. If you are going into this question,
do it thoroughly. Let us fix by law what is
fit to eat, and stick to it. I 'll back sauerkraut
before any dietary commission ever organized on
earth."

The council appointed a commission to conduct hearings and make a rigid code of laws
establishing the kind of foods for each meal.

Again Roland Adair, the Bard of Ramcat,
rose, shook his long hair and cleared his throat.

Norman lifted his hand for silence.

"I anticipate the poet's words. You solemnly
protest against the further establishment of a
tyranny which shall dare prescribe your food
from day to day. I grieve over the necessity of
these laws and mingle my tears with yours in
advance. But, in the language of a distinguished
citizen of the old republic, 'we are confronted
by a condition, not a theory.' The council stands
adjourned."

The Bard poured his bitter protest into

Catherine's patient ears and left with a growing conviction of her wisdom.

The woman with the drooping eyelids stood watching his retreating figure while a quiet smile of contempt played about her full, sensuous lips.

CHAPTER XX

THE UNCONVENTIONAL

WITHIN a week it was necessary to appoint a commission to formulate an elaborate code of laws regulating various nuisances which had developed in the community.

A kitchen-boy insisted on playing a cornet in his room. He did n't know a musical from a promissory note but he swore he 'd become a musician before he died. His efforts came near proving fatal to his neighbours before he was suppressed.

Several women had pet parrots. The people who lived near by strenuously objected. The parrots had to go.

A sailor had brought a monkey whose manners were not appreciated by any one except his master. The monkey had to go. Cats were arraigned for trial and a fierce battle raged over the question of allowing them in the building. The question was finally put to the popular vote in the assembly and the cats won by a good majority. But strict laws regulating the kind of cats, their number, and their care, were put into force.

Dogs won by a large majority when they were finally put on trial.

The commission on nuisances had finally to make a code of laws regulating table manners and the conduct of all social gatherings.

The one question which all but precipitated a civil war was the problem of dress. Inequality of wages meant, of necessity, inequality of dress.

A desperate effort was made by a large number to force the community to adopt a uniform for both men and women. It was fiercely opposed. Every woman who believed herself good looking refused to listen to any argument on the subject.

It was necessary at once, however, to formulate some sort of code. A number of men had been coming into the dining-room in their shirt sleeves. Some of them apparently never combed their hair or changed their linen. A number of women had gotten into the habit of coming into the dining-room in loose wrappers of variegated colors and without corsets.

The Bard of Ramcat was particularly severe in his public criticism of these women in the general assembly of the Brotherhood.

"In the name of beauty, I protest!" he cried. "Beauty is an attribute of God. It is woman's first duty to be beautiful, and if she is n't, at least to make man think she is. I insist that she shall have the widest liberty in the choice of dress. Only let her be careful that she is beautiful!"

The poet was heartily applauded, and a resolution was passed which embodied his ideas, approving the widest freedom of choice in dress, approving especially unconventional forms of dress, provided always the ideal of beauty was held inviolate.

In his speech advocating the immediate passage of the resolution the Bard urged every woman to outdo herself in the struggle for supreme beauty of appearance at the weekly ball on Friday evening.

His resolutions and speech bore surprising fruit.

When the festivities were at their height a crowd of fifteen pretty girls suddenly swept into the brilliantly lighted ball-room in tights! The sensation was so instantaneous and overwhelming the music stopped with a crash. The orchestra thought somebody had yelled fire.

The girls in their beautiful but unconventional dress tried to appear unconcerned. But even the Bard was appalled at the results.

The pretty young chorus-girls had taken him at his word. They had always cherished a secret desire to live in an unconventional real world, where they could have a chance to be themselves, without the hideous skirts of conventional society veiling their beauty. They had brought these costumes with them and joined the new moral world in the firm faith that their ideal would be realized. It had come very slowly, but it had come at last.

They donned their beautiful costumes with hearts fluttering in triumphant pride. But they had huddled into a corner of the ball-room in a panic of fright at the insane commotion their honest efforts to promote beauty had caused. One by one every woman in skirts save Barbara and Catherine left the room. The married ones seized their husbands and pushed them out ahead.

Norman, who was dancing with Barbara, broke down and burst into a paroxysm of laughter.

Some of the girls began to cry, but others made a brave effort to face the crowd of eager, giggling boys who pressed nearer.

The Bard approached with a serious look on his noble brow, deliberately put on his glasses and surveyed the crowd.

"My dear girls," he began, "I thank you from the bottom of my heart for the sincerity and honesty of your efforts to express beauty in unconventional form, but really this is beyond my wildest expectation."

Catherine drove the rude boys out of the room and closed the windows, while Barbara kissed the tears away from the hysterical innovators and led them back to their rooms.

The next morning the general assembly held an unusually solemn meeting at which it was voted by a large majority to settle at once and forever the question of dress by adopting a Socialist uniform of scarlet and white for the women, and for the men a dull gray suit with scarlet bands on the sleeve, a scarlet stripe and belt for the trousers.

The discussion was brief and Roland Adair, the Bard of Ramcat, protested in vain.

CHAPTER XXI

A PAIR OF COLD GRAY EYES

FROM the night of the ball at which the group of chorus-girls made their sensational entrance in tights, Norman had his hands full. Disorder had rapidly grown in the Brotherhood. Two distinct parties began to line up for a desperate struggle for supremacy, the one standing for the widest liberty of the individual members of the community, the other demanding the stern enforcement of law and order and the formulation of a complete and strict code of rules for the government of daily conduct.

Among the men assigned to various tasks there gradually appeared a number who slighted their work. From carelessness they drifted into utter incompetency and downright laziness. Groups of these loafers began to hang around the house daily.

When they had spent the last penny of their credit at the general store of the community, they began to steal. Not a day or night passed but complaints of thefts were made from every department of the colony. One of the most serious of these burglaries was the robbery of the winery of an enormous quantity of the most valuable wines.

Drunkenness had already become one of the serious problems of the Brotherhood, and the right to buy of the steward had been denied a large number of men and several women. These people began at once to show signs of intoxication. It was plain that the thieves had hidden this wine and that they were carrying on a secret traffic with those to whom it had been forbidden.

With the increase of reckless drunkenness another evil grew with alarming rapidity, the carousing of boisterous men and women. One of them very quickly passed the limits of tolerance. She was in many respects the most beautiful girl in the colony, barely nineteen years old, with luxuriant blond hair, and big, wide, staring baby-blue eyes. She had with it all a smile so saucy, so winsome, so elfish, and yet so innocent, it was impossible for the average man or woman to think ill of her. To every appeal of Barbara she merely showed her pretty white teeth in a winsome smile, promised her anything she asked, and proceeded to do as she liked.

At last her room was declared an intolerable nuisance by a committee appointed to enter the complaint on behalf of her neighbours on the floor on which she lived. The night before this committee appealed to Barbara two boys had fought a desperate fist duel in this room. The noise had roused the neighbours, and the case could no longer be ignored by the executive council.

Barbara was sent to this room with full power to deal with the offender.

"Good heavens," cried the girl, her big blue eyes opening wide with injured innocence, "how could I help it? They're both in love with me. I don't care a rap for either one of them, but they got to fighting, and I could n't stop them. I threw a pitcher of water on them, but they kept right on. I'd have called the police, but there was none to call. It was n't my fault."

"But my dear Blanche," pleaded Barbara, "can't you see that you are bringing scandal and disgrace into the colony?"

"It's not me!" the pretty lips pouted. "It's these old women who are talking. Let them shut their mouths and attend to their own business. I'm not bothering them."

"You deny the accusations they bring against your good name?" Barbara said, with some surprise.

"Of course I deny them," she snapped. "I've got to have some fun, have n't I? I can't help it that a dozen boys come to see me and nobody ever sees the old tabbies who lie about me, can I? I can't help it that they are old and ugly, can I?"

Barbara had ceased to listen to the glib tongue, whose lying chatter tired her. She looked about the room with increasing amazement. It was stuffed with presents of every conceivable description. Costly rugs adorned the floor. Soft pillows filled the couch by the window. Dainty and expensive works of art adorned her mantel, and the richest and most beautiful underwear lay in a smoothly laundered pile on her luxuriant bed.

"And how did you get all these costly and beautiful things, my dear?" Barbara asked, with a touch of sarcasm.

The big blue eyes opened wide again with wonder.

"Why, the boys who are in love with me gave them. Why should n't they? I can't help it that they are foolish, can I? God made them so."

"And you accepted these rich and costly things in perfect innocence of the evil meaning others might put on them?"

"Of course! How can I keep their tongues from wagging? Life's too short. I have but one life to live. I can't waste it worrying over nothing."

For the first time in her career Barbara stood face to face with naked evil — with a liar to whom a lie was good — a radiantly beautiful girl to whom shame was sweet.

For a moment the thought was suffocating. She looked out of the window at the infinite blue sea until the tears slowly blinded her. The first doubt of her theory of life crept into her heart and threw its shadow over the ideal of the new world she had built.

She took the girl's hand, slipped her arm around her neck, kissed the soft, shining hair, and sobbed:

"Poor little foolish sister! I'm afraid you've broken my heart to-day."

"I haven't done a thing! Honestly, I have n't!" the lusty young liar rattled on and on, in a hundred silly, vain protests, which Barbara never heard.

She left the room at length with a sickening sense of defeat, though the girl had promised her on the honour of her soul never again to give the slightest cause for complaint.

Many a day she had trudged through the streets of the great city, after hours of nerve-racking struggles with sin and shame and despair in the old world, but she had always come home at night with a heart singing a battle-hymn of victory. She knew the cause of all the pain, and she had given her life to right the wrong. Nothing daunted her, nothing disconcerted her. In the end triumph was sure, and while she felt this there could be no such thing as failure.

She stood before the full meeting of the executive council, honestly reported the case, and for the first time tasted the bitterness of defeat, helpless, complete, and overwhelming. While she was talking a peculiar expression in Wolf's cold gray eyes suddenly caught her attention and fixed her gaze on him with a curious fascination and horror. Wolf was quick to note her look, recovered himself and smiled in his old fatherly, friendly way.

"Don't worry, comrade. We've got to meet and settle such questions. They are merely the inheritance of civilization. It will take a little time, that's all."

But as Barbara's gaze lingered on the heavy brutal lines of Wolf's massive figure and she caught again the gleam of his gray eyes a sickening sense of foreboding gripped her heart.

CHAPTER XXII

THE FIGHTING INSTINCT

A S QUESTIONS of discipline became more and more pressing old Tom refused to sit as an active judge in the executive council.

Norman protested in vain against his decision to retire for a while.

"I can't do no good settin' thar listenin' to them fools," the miner declared. "They make me sick. Besides, ye all vote me down when I tells ye what to do, and things keep on goin' from bad to worse. Jest let me git out and move around among the boys a little. I think I can do some good. You folks is all too chicken-hearted to run this Brotherhood. Love and fellowship is all right, but ye 've got ter mix a little law and common sense before ye can straighten the kinks out of this here community."

Norman gave his consent reluctantly, and was amazed at the end of a week to observe a remarkable improvement in the spirit of the colony. Loafers disappeared, stealing all but ceased, drinking and fighting were on the decrease.

One by one old Tom had taken the loafers with

him on a long walk up the beach.   He was usually gone about an hour and always came back laughing and chatting with his friend in the best of humour. Invariably the loafer went to work.

In the same way he took a walk with each one of a crowd of wild, unmannerly boys, whose rudeness at the table and whose horse-play about the building had become unendurable. The effects of these walks seemed magical. Always the pair returned in a fine humour and the most marked revolution was immediately noted in the conduct of the offender.

Norman asked the old man again and again for the secret of his power.

He replied in the most casual way:

"Just had a plain heart-to-heart talk with 'em and told 'em what had to be — that's all."

The good work had continued for a week with uninterrupted success, when a bomb was suddenly exploded in the executive council by the appearance of an irate mother leading an insolent fourteen-year-old cub, who walked rather stiffly.

Amid a silence that was painful, the mother stripped the boy to the waist, thrust him before Norman and Barbara, and said:

"Now, tell them what you've just told me."

The boy glanced cautiously around to see if

his enemy were near and poured forth a tale the like of which had never been heard before.

"Old Tom asked me to take a walk with him. He got me away off in a lonely place behind the big rocks on that little island up the beach and pulled up a plank drawbridge so I could n't get back till he wanted to let me. He stripped me like this, tied me to a whipping-post and nearly beat the life out of me. He said he 'd been appointed by the council to settle with me in private so nobody would know anything about it."

"Said that he had been appointed by the council to whip you?" Norman asked, in amazement.

"That 's what he said, sir," the boy went on. "He gave me forty-nine lashes with a cowhide and then set down and talked to me a half hour."

"And what did he say?" Norman inquired, forcing back a smile by a desperate effort.

"He told me that he tried to get out of the work, but the council had forced it on him. Said there ought n't to be no hard feelings, that it was a dirty, tiresome job, and he did n't have no pleasure in it, but it had to be done for the salvation of the people. He said it was n't wise to talk about such things among the Brotherhood. I told him I 'd tell my ma the minute I got home. He said that would be foolish, that none of the others had said a word, that they had all taken their medicine like little men."

"He told you he had whipped all the others who had taken that walk with him ? " Norman gasped.

"That's what he said, sir," the boy insisted, "and I guess he had, for they'd pawed a hole in the sand 'round that whipping-post big enough to bury a horse in."

The boy paused and his mother shook him angrily.

"Tell what else he said to you!"

The cub glanced hastily toward the door and whispered:

"Said if I opened my mouth about what had happened he'd skin me alive."

The council sent the mother and son away with the assurance of immediate action.

The court adjourned and Norman started with Barbara at once to find Tom. Faithful to his new calling he had strolled up the beach with a man who once had been his partner as a prospector and miner. Joe Weatherby had been drinking heavily the week before and Tom had keenly felt the disgrace his old partner had brought on the Brotherhood by his rudeness in the dining-room.

Joe had thrown a plate of soup in the face of

a boy who was making facetious remarks about his capacity for strong drink. When rebuked by his neighbours he had accentuated his displeasure by overturning the table and smashing every dish on it. He ended the affair by roundly cursing the Brotherhood for its rules and regulations interfering with his personal liberty, threw his pack on his back, and struck the trail for the mountains to prospect for gold.

He had just returned, after a week's absence, and Tom seized the opportunity to invite Joe to take a walk with him.

Knowing the character of the two men, Norman felt quite sure this walk could not possibly have the usual happy ending that attended so many of these performances.

He quickened his pace.

"Hurry, or we may have a funeral for our next function," he cried, with a laugh.

A quarter of a mile up the beach the sound of loud angry words suddenly struck their ears from behind a pile of huge boulders.

"Quick, we 're just in time!" Barbara cried, "they 've begun to quarrel."

They cautiously approached the boulders and climbed to the top of the larger one overlooking the scene Tom had evidently chosen for his debate with Joe.

"Had n't you better part them now?" Barbara asked with some anxiety.

"No, I 'll stop them in time. I want to get acquainted with Tom's methods of persuasion first."

Tom 's voice was rising in accents of wrath. "Joe, I 'm a man o' peace — I 'm a member o' the Brotherhood and you 're my brother, but I 'll tell ye right now we 've got to have law and order in this community ——"

"And I say, Tom Mooney, there hain't no law exceptin' what 's inside a man."

"Yes, but how kin ye git any law inside a man ef he 's always chuck full er licker?"

"I don't drink to 'mount to nothin'," Joe protested. "Just a drop now an' then ter keep me in good health."

"Wall, ef you try any more capers in that dinin'-room, your health 's goin' ter break clean down — yer hear me?"

Joe eyed Tom a moment and said with sharp emphasis:

"I reckon I can take care o' myself, partner, without you settin' up nights to worry about me."

"That 's just the trouble, Joe, ye can't. You jined the Brotherhood, but yer faith 's gettin' weak. I 'm afeard you 're onregenerate, conceived in sin an' brought forth in iniquity, an' ye ain't had no change er heart nohow."

"Look here, what are ye drivin' at?" Joe asked, beginning to back away cautiously.

"I just want ter strengthen yer faith, partner," Tom protested kindly as he advanced good-naturedly and laid his hand on Joe's arm.

Joe shook it off and turned to go. With a sudden spring Tom was on him. A brief, fierce struggle ensued marked by low, savage growls like two bull-dogs clinched and searching for each other's throats.

"Stop them! Stop them! They'll kill one another," pleaded Barbara.

"No. It'll do them good. Wait," he replied, watching them breathlessly.

"Here! Here, you old fool," growled Joe. "Do you call this the Brotherhood of Man?"

"Yes, my son, and specially the Fatherhood er God. The Lord chastens them he loveth!"

With a sudden twist the writhing figures fell in the sand, Tom on top pinning Joe down.

Joe fought with fierce strength to rise but it was no use.

Tom clutched his throat and choked him steadily into submission.

"I'm er man o' peace, Joe," he repeated.

"Yes, you are!" the bottom one growled.

"But when I mingles with the unregenerate, my son, I trusts in God an' keeps my powder dry!"

"Let me up, you old fool!" Joe growled.

"Not yet, my son!" was the firm answer.

"You 'll get my dander up in a minute and some body's goin' ter git hurt," warned the prostrate figure.

"Please make them quit," Barbara whispered tremblingly.

"Nonsense. They 're enjoying themselves," Norman softly laughed.

"What are you tryin' ter do anyhow?" whined Joe.

"I 'm callin' a lost sinner to repentance," was the prompt answer.

"Lemme up, I tell ye," Joe yelled, struggling with desperation.

Tom choked him again into silence and seated himself comfortably across Joe's stomach.

"Now, Joseph, my boy. I want you ter say over the catechism of the Brotherhood of Man. Hit 'll freshen yer mind an' be good fer yer soul ——"

Another grim struggle interrupted the teacher.

"Say it after me: I believe in the fatherhood er God ——"

Joe squirmed.

"Say it!"

Still no sound. Tom firmly gripped his throat and Joe gurgled:

"Fatherhood er God!"

"And brotherhood o' man!"

"Brotherhood er man!"

"Yer believe it now?" Tom fiercely asked.

Joe feebly assented.

Tom gripped his throat.

"Say it strong!"

"Yes — I believe it!" Joe confessed.

Again the under man struggled desperately and the man on top fiercely choked him into a quieter frame of mind.

"Now again: No drunkard shall inherit the kingdom er God!"

Joe repeated, "No drunkard — shall — what?"

"Inherit—the—kingdom—er God—by golly you 've forgot yer Bible too!"

"Inherit — the — kingdom er — God!"

"Who shall not inherit the kingdom of God?"

"No drunkard!" Joe answered.

"Let that soak into yer lost soul!" Tom growled, pausing a moment.

"Now once more! Bear—ye—one—another's burdens!"

Joe hesitated and the man on top bumped the words out of him one at a time:

"Bear —ye — one — another's — burdens!"

"An' ye're goin' ter help me bear mine?" the teacher asked.

"Ain't I a-doin' it now?" grumbled the man below.

"Well, once more then: Private property is theft!"

"That's a lie an' you know it," Joe sneered.

"The big chief says so and it goes — say it!"

"Private property is theft," Joe repeated.

"Well, then, once more: Love — one — another!"

"Love one another," came the feeble echo.

"Do ye love me?" Tom fiercely inquired.

Joe struggled.

"Say it!" commanded the teacher.

"I love ye," he groaned.

Norman suddenly appeared on the scene followed by Barbara and the two miners leaped to their feet.

"Tom, old boy," the young leader cried, "you mean well, but we are told by the preacher that the kingdom of God cometh not of observation — it must be from within."

"Just goin' over his Sunday-school lesson with him, Chief."

Joe made a hostile movement, and Norman stepped between them.

"Come! You two big kids — enough of this now, shake hands and make up!"

The men both hung back stubbornly.

Norman turned to Tom.

"Were you not partners and friends before you joined the Brotherhood?"

"Yes," the old miner replied grudgingly. "We bin tergether twelve years an' we worked an' played tergether, starved an' froze tergether, lived tergether, an' slept under the same blanket — he's the only partner I ever had — an' he's my best friend" — Tom paused and choked — "but I don't like 'im!"

"Shake hands and make up!" Barbara laughed.

They hung back a moment longer until Barbara's smile became resistless.

Joe extended his hand, exclaiming:

"Shake, you old coyote!"

Norman gave Joe a serious talk — got a pledge from him to quit drink and stand by him in his efforts to bring order out of the confusion and chaos in which the colony was floundering.

"You think I can do anything to help you?" Joe asked incredulously.

"Of course you can. You and Tom are two men I've known all my life. I know where to find you if I get into trouble."

"Is there goin' ter be any trouble?" Tom broke in, eagerly.

"Not yet, but it's coming. When it does we'll

fight it out and win. I 've set my life on the issue of this experiment."

Joe extended him his hand. "I 'm sorry I got drunk. I won't do it again — we 'll stand by ye!"

"Through thick an' thin," Tom added.

"And hereafter, Tom," Norman said with a smile, "I 'd like to be consulted before you hold any more sessions of your court up the beach."

Tom started.

"You 've heard about it?"

"Yes."

"By gum, I knowed I oughter licked that kid again!" the old miner observed, regretfully.

Norman, said gravely: "Tom, we are getting into deep water. I 've begun to have some doubts about our safety. A leader must lead. And I 'm going to do it. Can I depend on you to execute my orders and mine alone?"

"Every day in the year," was the firm reply.

"The same here," Joe echoed.

Barbara had drawn apart from the group of men and stood watching them with keen, suspicious interest as the two miners started homeward with restored good humour.

"What did you mean by saying that you were afraid of coming trouble?" Barbara eagerly asked of Norman. "What have you heard? What do you suspect?"

"Nothing," he answered, thoughtfully. "But I've had the blues for a week. It's been growing on me that we are not getting on except into situations more and more impossible. There's a screw loose somewhere in our system. There's going to be a wreck unless we find and repair it."

"I have felt this, too, and I think I know the cause."

"What?"

"Liberty which has degenerated into licence. We lack authority and the power to enforce it."

"And this is the one thing we cursed in the old system — the law, power, authority."

"No," Barbara quickly objected. "We did not rebel against law or the exercise of authority. We rebelled against its unjust use."

"And what depresses me is that I am convinced that we must use the power of law with more stern, direct, and personal pressure than ever known under the system of capitalism, or we must fail."

"Is not such pressure desirable?"

"It depends on who applies the pressure — but it seems inevitable — and it depresses me."

Barbara broke into a joyous laugh.

"Away with gloomy forebodings! It's only a day's fog. It will lift. The sun is shining behind it now."

Her laughter was contagious. Norman smiled

ın quick sympathy, and a response of hope and courage was just forming itself on his lips when he looked toward the house and saw an excited crowd packed in the doorway.

"What on earth is the matter?" Barbara gasped.

"Some accident has happened," he replied, quickly. "Come, we must hurry!"

Catherine's lithe figure darted down the steps and met them on the lawn.

"What is it?" Norman cried.

"A murder!"

"A murder?" Barbara repeated, incredulously.

"Yes — wilful, deliberate, cruel, horrible!" Catherine went on excitedly.

"Not old Tom and Joe?" Norman broke in.

"No — Blanche ——"

"Oh, God, I knew it," Barbara gasped. "Go on."

"Blanche kept on playing fast and loose with the two boys who fought over her the other night. George Mann found his rival in her room just now, waylaid him in the hall, and when he came out sprang on him like a fiend, stabbed him through the heart and cut his throat. The brothers of the dead boy swear they will kill the murderer on sight, and they've locked him in your room, Norman, for safety. The men are excited to frenzy. Nobody likes the boy who did the crime. The rougher ones swear they are going to hang him. They tried to break in your door twice, but Herman knocked the ringleaders down and with Tom and Joe beat the crowd back. Something must be done at once to prevent another outbreak."

Norman hurried to the scene and joined Wolf in his defence of the prisoner. Tom formed a guard of ten men heavily armed and marched the prisoner to the top of the house, placed him in the small room in one of the central towers, and stationed one man inside and five on the stairway leading into the tower.

The executive council met immediately and voted unanimously to erect a prison, establish a penal colony on the small island at the north of Ventura, and restore the whipping-post for minor offenders.

The announcement of this momentous act was made to the general assembly without request for debate or an expression of opinion. It was received in silence.

The Bard could not protest. He was still confined to his room from the effects of a recent argument with his wife.

CHAPTER XXIII

THE CORDS TIGHTEN

ON WOLF'S urgent advice Norman determined to use the autocratic power invested in him by the deed of gift to establish a complete code of law and enforce it without fear or favour. As the cords tightened, scores who became dissatisfied with their lot offered their resignations and asked to return to their old homes.

In answer to their clamour Norman posted this notice on the bulletin board:

"Every member of the army of the Brotherhood of Man enlisted for five years' service. Resignations will not be considered and deserters will be tried by court-martial. I am going to use my power for the best interests of the Brotherhood. I ask the cooperation of all the loyal members of the colony. Of traitors I ask no quarter, and I expect to give none.

"NORMAN WORTH,
"Trustee and General Manager."

The effects of the proclamation were instantaneous. The helplessness of any attempt to resist authority firmly established under such daring leadership was at once apparent to the most stupid mind.

Loafing, drinking, stealing, carousing, and disorder of all kind were reduced at once to a minimum.

One act, however, of the executive council under Norman's direction precipitated a storm in an unexpected quarter.

The council removed Blanche and a group of wayward girls with whom she associated to a cottage outside the lawn.

The women of the Brotherhood were practically unanimous in their demands that the whole group be immediately expelled from the colony. A committee of three aggressive women presented their demand to Norman in no uncertain language.

His reply was equally emphatic:

"Comrades," he said, firmly, "I shall do nothing of the kind. We are going to work out this experiment in human society without compromise. We have successfully cut communication with the outside world. The crew of our ship are no longer allowed to land and only picked men unload her cargo. We are not going to play the baby act and dump these girls back on the old civilization which we have denounced. They may be wayward but they are our sisters."

"They are not mine," shouted one of the committee. "The brazen creatures! And we do not propose to have our sons and daughters corrupted by association with them."

"Then we must find some other solution than that of transportation," Norman insisted.

"Send them to the penal colony, then," demanded the committee.

"And back in a circle we immediately travel to the crimes of civilization from which we fled. I prefer to send the boys who associate with them. They are the real offenders."

"I deny that assertion," firmly declared the leader of the committee. "My boy is one of the unfortunate victims of these brazen wretches. Before we came to this island he never gave me a word of impudence. From the night he met Blanche at our first ball he was beyond my advice or control. These girls are the enemies of society and this colony cannot exist if they remain within its life."

"I refuse to believe it," Norman cried, with scorn. "It is your duty to reform these girls and restore them to mental and physical sanity, and as the leader of this colony I direct you to take up this divine work."

"And I, for one," spoke, for the first time, the silent gray-haired member of the committee, "refuse to smirch my hands with the task."

Norman, looked into the calm face of this white-haired, motherly looking woman with amazement.

"I can't understand you, comrade mother!" he exclaimed, with bitterness.

"That's because you're young, handsome, inexperienced, and, above all, because you are a man," was the quick reply. "I have spent a busy life since my own children grew out of the home nest in New York City in trying to help other people's children less fortunate than my own. I've helped scores of boys and never had one to disappoint me yet. I've tried to help scores of girls of the type we are discussing. I've always regretted it. I found them shallow, false, lazy, stupid, worthless. I have never looked at one of them except to blush that I am a woman. I speak from the saddest and most hopeless experiences of my life."

Norman cut the argument short with a gesture of angry impatience. "This discussion is a waste of breath. As long as I am in command of this colony no such insane act of injustice shall be committed against these girls."

"Then it's time you gave place to a man of greater wisdom and less sentimental mush in his brain," replied the calm, gray-haired woman.

"Thank you," the young leader replied, with chilling politeness, "you may be right — but in the meantime I accept the responsibility. Good day."

He had made three enemies whose power he was soon to feel. As they passed through the doorway Catherine greeted them politely and soothed their ruffled spirits with gentle words.

CHAPTER XXIV

SOME INTERROGATION POINTS

THE establishment of a police and detective service completed the efficient organization of the colony. Its life now began to move with clock-like regularity.

But these changes were not made without provoking fierce debates and bitter prophecies in the general assembly over which Norman presided every Friday night.

He began to listen to these endless wrangles, however, with a sense of growing anger. It became clearer each week that they were the source of cliques and factions, of plots and counter-plots, within the colony. His patience reached the limit on the night he announced the completion of the jail.

"This is a sad present I am forced to make you to-night, comrades," he said, with a note of weariness in his voice. "But I have no choice in the matter. It was forced on the executive council. Crimes were committed which threatened the existence of our society. We had to meet the issue squarely. We could have begged the question by calling in the authorities of the State of California, acknowledged our defeat, and surrendered. We are not ready to surrender. We have n't begun to fight yet."

He had scarcely taken his seat when Diggs, the human interrogation-point, slowly unwound his lank figure, adjusted his eye-glasses, and gazed smilingly at the chairman.

Norman squirmed with rage as the glint of light from Diggs's big lenses began to irritate his spirit.

Barbara slipped her little hand under the table and found his. He clasped it gratefully and refused to let go. She allowed him to hold it a minute and drew it away laughing.

"Comrades," the man of questions slowly began, "we are making rapid progress. Our new building will soon be finished and another colony of two thousand enthusiastic souls will be added to our commonwealth. If we are going to successfully carry on this work we must begin to develop with infinite patience the details of this larger life.

"I submit to you some questions that are profoundly interesting to me.

"How are we to prevent speculation, wages being unequal? How is one community to exchange products with another? How determine which line of goods each community shall make?

"What is to be done with a strong minority who are bitterly opposed to the action of the majority when we assume our permanent democratic form?

"How are the thousand and one matters pertaining to private life and habits to be settled without continually augmenting the power of government? The authority of the most absolute despot who ever lived never dared to sit on questions we must decide. Can we do it?

"If we are ever to attain a condition of equality must we not forbid gifts and exchanges? For, if men are not to be allowed to grow rich by trading, must not the State forbid private exchanges of every nature?

"On the other hand, if the State alone can make exchanges, how can we prevent a shrewd man from getting rich by dealing with the State itself?

"If the State will not make exchanges, what is one to do who has taken a piece of property and finds later he has no use for it? For example: if Miss Blanche grows tired of looking at her piano, which she cannot play, and desires to exchange it for a carriage and pair of horses, must she continue to walk because she cannot effect the exchange?

"If we solve these troubles by declaring all property in common, who shall decide the privilege

BARBARA.

of use which the various tastes of individuals may demand ?

"If each member be allowed a fixed number of units of value for each day of the year, must he spend them at once, or will the State keep an account for each individual ? If he does n't spend all his allowance by the end of the year can he save it and thus accumulate a private fortune ?

"Or will the State force him to spend all, thus encouraging reckless habits ?

"Suppose that a spendthrift squanders his allowance at once and later breaks his leg, has it amputated, and needs a hundred dollars to buy a wooden leg, how will he get it ? Will the State make good his recklessness, force him to buy his own leg, or make him hop through the year on one leg ?"

"I move we adjourn!" Joe yelled, from the rear.

"Second the motion!" Tom echoed, from the front.

The Bard, who had recovered sufficiently to attend on crutches, rose painfully, adjusted the bandage on his eye, and once more raised his voice in protest.

"I demand freedom of speech on behalf of my friend whom those rowdies are insulting!" he thundered.

With reluctance the chairman rapped for order,

and Diggs wiped his glasses and smilingly proceeded:

"We have established a general nursery for the children. As they grow up, who shall decide at what age each child shall begin to work? Some children are slow, some quick in growth. Will the new State of Ventura take direct charge of all children?

"Or, supposing that separate families are allowed to live apart and parents to govern their own children, how is each child to be protected so that it gets its exact due? How is it to be known whether the parents misappropriate the fund of a child, or favour one more than another?

"As our numbers increase we cannot avoid the religious question."

"Amen, O Lord!" shouted Methodist John.

"A number of good people are clamouring for the use of this hall for religious services every night. We may deny their demands now. But we cannot as they increase. How are we to meet them? Shall we tax the unbeliever to support a church? Or shall we tax the believer to pay for lighting this hall for a weekly ball?

"If religion is allowed, who shall determine how many preachers each denomination can have? How many sisters shall be allowed the Catholics and how many monks, and how shall they be distributed? To whom shall they answer, the State, or their superior church dignitary?

"Shall Protestants be allowed a sum equal to the amount used in support of religious orders? If so, who shall determine how it shall be expended?

"If churches are built, who shall determine their cost and their style of architecture if the State erects them?

"When our theatre is opened, shall admission be free? If not, what shall be done when the receipts fall below expenses?

"What compensation can we give to those who hate theatres? If a small majority want a dance-hall and musical extravaganza, and a minority want only the serious drama, which shall it be? Suppose a majority demand a race-course? Shall the resources of the colony be used thus against the bitter protest of those who do not believe in racing? Suppose, just before the race-course is finished, the majority become a minority and the work is stopped — has the new majority the right to destroy the property and accumulate a new fund for a different purpose?

"Must a doctor always come when he's called — even for imaginary, hysterical, and foolish causes? Will the people vote for and elect their own doctor, or will he be assigned? If the doctor proves a failure, how will they get rid of him? If they get rid of him, how can he be saddled on another community? Shall one community suffer at the hands of an incompetent man, while a physician of genius ministers to the one next door? If a great surgeon is needed by ten persons at the same hour, who shall decide which operation he shall perform, and who shall live or die in consequence?

"Who shall say when a doctor is not fit to practise?

"We have just established a weekly paper. Within a year the population will need a daily. Who shall say when an editor is competent?

"Some men fail in early life and make their great success later. At what period, or after how long a trial, shall it be decided that a man is a failure and must quit his chosen or assigned work?

"Many young men promise well at first and make later miserable failures. Many are failures at first and make great successes. Who shall decide which to continue and which to stop? If a youth is forced to abandon a work on which he has set his heart, how can he be made of service to the community in a work he loathes?

"We must continue to make inventions, or progress ceases. When the cost of experiments is greater than the total income of a citizen, how can the inventor bear the expense? Will any man sacrifice his own funds and his own time on an uncertain experiment when he can receive no benefit from the work?

"Many men are working now over problems all other men believe cannot be solved. If the State must furnish the capital to make the experiments of inventors, who will be responsible for the enormous waste of treasure on senseless and useless and impossible inventions?

"Who can decide whether ideas proposed are useless or impossible? All great inventions which have revolutionized the history of ages have been laughed at by the world.

"How can we punish the jobbery and waste and corruption which may enter from experiments which are not made in good faith? Cannot any group of shrewd men pretend to have invented a machine which will save over half the labour of the colony, and spend millions on this imaginary invention which proves useless? If such an abuse of power should be made, would not the effect be to end forever all experiments and stop the progress of the world?

"When many cities have been built and one is more healthful, beautiful, and cultured than the others, shall those who live in the poorer cities be allowed to move or be forced to remain where they are? How are sculptors, artists, musicians, or architects to be apportioned among different communities? Suppose they all demand the right to live in one place?

"Will the State publish all books by all authors, or will selections be made? If all books are published will not vast sums be wasted in printing worthless trash? If selections are made, what unprejudiced, infallible board can be found competent to decide?

"If a man chooses to be a writer, how many years shall he be allowed to work at his occupation if in the opinion of the judges he shows no talent?

"Will the State permit freedom of opinion in the columns of its papers and the books printed? If so, what shall hinder a treasonable conspiracy from destroying respect for its authority? If opinions are to be edited by the State, how can the freedom of the press be maintained?

"What shall be done with the Negro, the Chinaman, and the Indian when their numbers largely increase? Will these inferior races be placed on an absolute equality with the Aryan and will they be allowed to freely intermarry? If so, can the new mongrel race maintain itself against the progress and power of the great high-bred races of men?

"Are women to receive the same allowance as men, and married women the same as spinsters?

"Shall men and women be required to marry

or be allowed to remain single? Shall all women be made to work? If it continues to cost more to support a single woman than a married one, how can equality of rights be maintained?

"As food is the basis of all supply, many must be farmers. How shall this great industry be conducted ultimately? Can we allow individuals to work small farms? If so, who determines the kind of crop each farm shall raise? How much land will a man be required to work?

"An Italian from the north of Italy can raise more on one acre than an Irishman can on ten —whose method shall be used, and whose capacity be taken for the standard?

"How many hours shall constitute a day on the farm? Shall a farmhand get only a dollar a day and a bricklayer two? If so, where is the justice and equality of such an arrangement?

"Can a farmer be allowed vacations? If so, must he ask permission where to go? If not, suppose he goes at seedtime or harvest, gets drunk, stays two weeks or two months, and destroys a year's crop? Who shall pay for this enormous damage, and how shall the penalty be enforced?

"Suppose a poor manager spoils the crop on an immense tract of land, how can any adequate penalty be enforced?

"Shall one general manager decide what kind of crops to raise on each piece of land or each manager decide for himself? Suppose they all raise hay ——"

"Then you 'll have plenty to eat the balance of your life — you and all the other jackasses in the colony!" old Tom growled.

A laugh rippled the crowd and the speaker paused in angry confusion. For the first time he lost his temper and stood glaring at his tormentors in silent rage.

Norman whispered to Barbara:

"Wolf has urged me for some time to suppress this meeting. Shall I do it?"

"Yes. It 's a nuisance. I agree with him. Do it."

Norman rose just as Diggs sat down choking with anger.

"Comrades," the young leader said, in commanding tones. "I think this assembly has completed its work of discussion. The questions propounded here to-night are important. We will meet and solve them in due time, as we come to them. What this community needs now is the spirit of coöperation, of loyalty, and industry. We have been assigned our tasks for the year. Now every man to his work! We have had enough of wrangling and questioning.

Let's live and breathe awhile. The executive council has decided to close the weekly sessions of the assembly until the annual election of officers next spring. Hereafter a musicale and dance will be held both Monday and Friday evenings."

The young folks broke into hearty applause led by old Tom and his partner Joe.

The Bard sprang to his feet, his one good eye blazing with inspired wrath.

"And I denounce this act of tyranny as the climax of a series of infamies! You have now forged the chains of slavery on every limb. Free speech has been suppressed — in God's name, what next?"

But the crowd only laughed. The Bard had protested so often his words ceased to have weight. The halo of romance that once wreathed his classic brow had faded with the painful dis-illusioning which followed a thrashing his wife had given him. He was a prophet without honour and his warnings fell on deaf ears.

Wolf and Catherine stood at the door with a word of cheer, a friendly nod, or a silent pressure of the hand for every one who emerged from the hall. These two alone at every turn grew in prestige among all jarring factions of the struggling colony.

CHAPTER XXV

THE MASTER HAND

THE whole machinery of the colony responded instantly to the grip of the master's hand. It was the one thing needed to insure successful progress.

When the Brotherhood realized that the young poet-athlete was not merely a love-sick dreamer and theorist, but a man of quick decisions, of firm and inflexible will, and the power to execute his will, they fell in line, caught the step, and order emerged from chaos.

When a crisis called for decision he made it with lightning rapidity and stuck to it. The situation demanded a dictatorship for the moment, and he did not hesitate to assume it. He saw before him sure success. If fools and cranks interfered with his plans he would crush and push them aside. The consciousness of power and its daily exercise developed his faculties to their highest tension. His mind began to arrange every detail of the vast and complicated system of the new social scheme. Men became the mere tools with which he would work out the revolution in human society. Every scrap of knowledge he had ever gained flashed through his excited imagination and fell into its place in the creation of the new order.

He put the machine-shops to work constructing the big gold dredge on which he had experimented one summer.

He had a pet scheme of farming which had come into his mind from watching his father's gardener the year before raise the most delicious cantaloups he had ever tasted. He discovered the secret of their marvellous sweetness and leaped to an instantaneous conclusion. He had the opportunity to test this inspiration now on a scale as vast as his dreams.

He called the superintendents and overseers of the farm together, and asked their plans for the crop on the five hundred acres of fertile lands under cultivation. They gave him their schedule for a variety of crops.

"Won't this soil grow cantaloups?" he asked.

They all reported that it would.

"Then I suggest that the entire acreage be planted in these vines."

To a man they declared the plan absurd.

"But suppose," he persisted, "that we raise and send to the East the most delicious melon they have ever tasted, and suppose we get three dollars a crate, we will make three hundred dollars an acre and our first crop will be worth one hundred and fifty thousand dollars."

They laughed at him.

"Do you know," smilingly inquired the superintendent, "how much it will cost to plant and harvest such a crop?"

"I should say twenty-five dollars an acre," he replied.

"Double it," he cried.

"Very well, fifty dollars an acre," Norman agreed. "In round numbers it will cost us twenty-five thousand dollars. That leaves a profit of more than a hundred thousand, does n't it?"

Again the superintendent laughed.

"And would you risk this enormous sum on one experiment? Suppose your melons would not be sweet?"

"There is no such possibility," the young enthusiast declared. "Their sweetness depends solely on two things — the quality of the seed and the quantity of rain which falls on them while they are growing. We are wasting a supreme opportunity. No rain falls in Ventura during the summer. We get our water to the roots by irrigation, not by rainfall. Get the right seed and your melons must be perfect. This is a scientific fact I have seen demonstrated. Try it on a vast scale and success is sure."

They voted unanimously against the proposition. Norman insisted. The superintendent resigned and appealed to the executive council. Wolf and Catherine, Tom and Barbara advised against placing so much capital in a single enterprise.

"I 've got to make you rich and successful in spite of yourselves," Norman finally declared. "For the present I control these funds and I 'm going to plant this crop. So that settles it. I 'm sorry we can't agree."

His instantaneous decision fairly took Wolf's breath.

Barbara laughed and congratulated him.

"At least you have the courage of your convictions. I can't help admiring it."

As further opposition was useless, the order was put into execution. The superintendent finally caught the young man's spirit, withdrew his resignation, and undertook the work with enthusiasm.

At the end of the summer the success of the colony was astounding. The wildest prediction of the young leader fell below the facts. The crop of cantaloups averaged one hundred and five crates to the acre, and brought three dollars and a half a crate. The net profit on the melons reached the enormous total of one hundred and fifty thousand dollars.

The men who raised the crop and added this wealth to the treasury of the colony were not slow in demanding an immediate readjustment of the scale of wages.

Two hundred and fifty men had done all the work of planting, cultivating, harvesting this crop and added ten times as much to the year's income as the combined labour of all the other members of the colony.

Brick-masons were receiving two dollars a day and farm-hands one dollar. The miners who were digging for gold in the mountain ranges and on the beaches were receiving five dollars a day and had added as yet not a single dollar to the wealth of the community. They had discovered gold in three new districts and thousands of dollars had been wasted in vain efforts to make it pay. The farmers protested bitterly against such waste, and demanded the equalization of wages.

Their spokesman astonished Norman by the vehemence and audacity of their demands:

"If Socialism means justice," he shouted, "now is the time to prove it! Labour creates all value. We have created one hundred and fifty thousand dollars' worth of wealth for the colony and we have received a mere pittance. If we created this wealth ——"

"Wait a minute, comrades," Norman interrupted, with irritation. "Why should you continue to repeat that foolish assertion? You did n't create this wealth."

"Then I 'd like to know who did?" shouted the orator. "We turned the soil, placed the fertilizers, planted every seed, cultivated every vine, pulled every melon, packed and placed them on the steamer. If we did n't make the wealth, who did?"

"I did," the young leader declared. "I conceived the possibility of this crop. I tried to persuade your superintendent and overseers. They had no faith. I forced them to plant these particular seeds against their own wishes. Your labour is a fixed thing year in and year out. All men must work or die. All life is a struggle thus with tooth and nail for a living. The creator of wealth is the superior intelligence that conceives something better than this clodhopper's daily task. You did what you were told to do. Your hands would have worked just as many hours at labour just as tiresome over a crop of beans that would n't have paid a profit at all this year. Wealth belongs to its creator. I made the crop, your hands were the mere automata which my brain directed.

Your demands are absurd. I refuse to consider them or to permit their discussion."

The farmers refused point-blank to submit to this decision, and voted unanimously to quit work until they were given justice. Every plough stopped and the entire machinery of food production came to a dead standstill.

Norman threatened to refuse them admission to the dining-hall unless they returned to work, and they boldly replied that they would smash the door down and take what was their own.

Had the farmers been alone in their demands for an equalization of wages, the situation would have been easier to handle. But discontent over the question of wages had been growing steadily since the day of the decision that wages should be unequal.

The distinctions of wealth and poverty were rapidly making their appearance as in the old world. The cook had married a scrubwoman and the scrubwoman's daughter had married the drainman who had charge of the sewers. The combine income of the two highest-salaried workers in the colony had at once formed the nucleus of a new aristocracy of wealth.

The strike of the entire farming division of the colony was the match thrown in the powder magazine. Discontent flamed in every department of labour.

The demand for absolute equality of wages became resistless. It was the only thing which could once more bring order out of chaos.

Norman called a meeting of the general assembly and submitted the question for their discussion and decision. The debate was long, fierce, and bitter. In vain did the young leader plead with those who were receiving the highest rates that the profits of the colony would be greater and that each would share alike in the total wealth of the community. They denounced the proposed act as the climax of infamy.

The chef was furious.

"You give me the wages of a clodhopper and ask me to prepare a table fit for a king. Well, try it, and see what you get."

He sat down repeating his threat in a series of endless announcements to the people around him.

"I think he'll poison us all if you pass this law," Barbara whispered.

"The farmers will run us through with their pitchforks if we don't," he laughed.

"Poisoning is the easier way," she sighed.

The leader of the brass band raised the biggest row of all. From the first these men had refused to lift their hand to do a thing except to play at stated hours each day and furnish the music for the three evenings of social amusement.

"You place me on an equality with the lout who holds a calf or the clodhopper who holds a plough — I, who feed the soul with ravishing melody — I, who lift man from earth to heaven on the wings of angels!" The band leader swelled with righteous wrath and sat down beside the cook who was still muttering incoherently:

"Let 'em try it — and see what they get!"

Yet, in spite of the fierce threats of the cook, the scrubwoman, the drainman, the musician, and all the high-salaried favourites of labour, the inevitable occurred. When put to a vote equal wages were established by an overwhelming majority.

Each member of the colony, man, woman, and child, was voted free food, clothes, and shelter, and a credit of five hundred dollars a year at the Brotherhood store.

The executive council was abolished and in its place a board of governors established, composed of the heads of each department of labour and presided over by two regents, a man and a woman, elected by the general assembly. Norman and Barbara were elected regents without opposition, and the old heads of each department of labour placed on the board of governors to serve until the approaching annual election.

The assembly proposed:

"Article I. of the constitution of the new State of Ventura as follows:

"Every citizen of the State must labour according to his ability. Those who can work and will not shall be made to work."

No man who voted this simple and obviously just law could dream of the tremendous results. It was merely the enactment into statutory law of the first principle of an effective Socialism:

"From every man according to his ability, unto every man according to his needs."

The first obvious requirement of such a law was an immediate increase of the police and detective force at the command of the regents and the board of governors.

Norman thanked the assembly for the promptness and thoroughness which had characterized their work, and closed his congratulations with a sentence of peculiarly sinister meaning to the man who had ears to hear.

"Hereafter, comrades, we can move forward without another pause. There can never be another strike on the island of Ventura. The State is now supreme."

The Wolfs, who had modestly declined all office,

were omnipresent during the long sessions of the assembly, which had lasted two days. Everywhere they had counselled compromise, forbearance, good fellowship, moving quietly from group to group in the big hall, and always winning new friends.

Wolf's gnarled hand gripped Norman's at the close of the meeting as he bent his massive head and whispered:

"A great day's work, Comrade Chief — one that will make history."

The young leader's face clouded as he slowly replied:

"I wish I were sure that it will be history of the right kind."

"You doubt it?" the old leader asked incredulously.

"It all depends on our leadership."

"With your hand on the helm" — Wolf paused and smiled curiously — "the ship of State is safe."

CHAPTER XXVI

AT THE PARTING OF THE WAYS

AGAIN the colony entered on a period of active and efficient industry. Every man was at his post and did the work assigned him.

Eight hours was fixed as a working day in all departments. The first acts of insubordination were promptly suppressed. The discipline of an army was strictly enforced — the guard-house and whipping-post were found sufficient.

No report except the most favourable had ever reached the outside world, and thousands of applicants in San Francisco were clamouring for admission. The new colony house with accommodation for two thousand had been completed, and another of like size was under way.

Wolf had urged Norman to admit a new colony at once and prepare for the third. But the difficulties of government and the fights within the Brotherhood had alarmed the young leader. He hesitated, and the big new building as yet remained empty.

As the day for the annual meeting of the assembly drew near, doubts of the future grew darker in the young regent's mind. He had the power, under the deed of gift, to prolong the experiment another year, holding the title to the property for further experiment, or divide the profits between the members and reconvey the gift back to its donors, or by deed convey at once the whole property to the Brotherhood and end his trusteeship.

Which should it be?

His faith in his fellow man had been shaken by the events of the past year, and yet the colony had succeeded. Its wealth was great and its prospects greater. With the perfect discipline recently inaugurated and wisely administered, no limit could be fixed to the productive power of such an organization.

That he should hesitate a moment after the achievements of the year was a stunning shock to Wolf. The moment he realized the import of the crisis, he at once appealed to Barbara.

"You alone can save us, child," he urged. "You must act at once. You promised to lead him captive in your train. You have failed for one reason only ——"

"Yes, I know," Barbara interrupted. "I have n't tried. I confess it."

"There is not a moment to lose," Wolf urged. "We are entering on the most wonderful development in the history of the human race. The only thing lacking for its triumphant achievement is faith and leadership. Secure from our young dreamer the title to this island and you will achieve an immortal deed — you will not hesitate or fail?"

"No," was the firm answer. "I will not fail. I 'm going with him to-day on a mountain climb. Just for fun, if for nothing else, I 'll test my power."

"You 'll report to me the moment you return?" Wolf urged.

"Yes," she answered, dreamily.

Norman found Barbara in a mood resistlessly charming. She seemed to have utterly forgotten that she was grown up or had ever been the herald of a revolutionary cause. She was a laughing girl of eighteen again, with the joy of youth sparkling in her eyes and laughter ringing in every accent of her voice.

Instantly the mood of the man reflected hers. He threw to the winds the cares and worries of the great adventure that had brought them together, and the island of Ventura became the enchanted isle of song and story.

"We shall be just two children to-day — shall we not?" she asked.

"Yes," he responded gaily, "two children who have run away from school, tired of books, with hearts hungry for the breath of the fields."

For half an hour hill and dale rang with laughter as they ascended the path of the brook. They came to a wide expanse of still water. And Norman said with a bantering laugh:

"We leave the stream here and climb the hill to the left. I must wade and carry you across this place if you 're not afraid ?"

"Who 's afraid ?" she asked with scorn.

"All right."

He removed his shoes, and rolled his trousers high.

"Now your arm around my neck, and no jumping or screaming until we 're safe on the other shore."

She hesitated just an instant, blushed, and slipped her soft round arm about his neck as he lifted her slight figure and began to pick his way across the treacherous surface of the slippery bottom. His foot slipped on a muddy stone. She gave a scream, and both arms gripped his neck in sudden fear. Her burning cheek pressed his forehead.

"I beg your pardon," she cried, blushing red. "I did n't mean to smother you."

"And I distinctly said no jumping or screaming, did n't I ?"

"I won't do it again — oh, dear!"

Again both arms clasped his neck in a strangling,

smothering hug, which he purposely prolonged with an extra slip which might have been avoided.

Her face was scarlet now and the blushes refused to go. They lingered in great red bunches after he had carefully placed her on the smooth grass on the opposite bank.

"Honestly, I'm afraid I disgraced myself, did n't I?" she asked, timidly.

"No. It was all my fault," he replied. "I did it on purpose."

"Perhaps I choked you on purpose, too!" she answered, blushing again.

Norman looked at her thoughtfully.

"You know I never saw you blush before. I like it."

"Is it becoming?" she asked, demurely.

"Very."

"You know I was never in a man's arms before."

"And you did n't like it?" he asked, with a smile playing around his mouth.

"To tell you the truth, I found it very awkward."

"Awkward?" he laughed.

"And exciting," she confessed.

"Shall we repeat it until you are used to it?"

"Thank you, I'm sufficiently amused for to-day," she answered, soberly. "And now we will put on our shoes and be good children."

For the rest of the journey Norman found her strangely silent. Now and then he caught her looking at him furtively out of her big brown eyes, as if she had just met him and was half afraid to go further.

He found himself particularly sensitive to her moods. The moment she became silent and thoughtful her impulses ruled his, and not a word was spoken for a mile. Scarcely two sentences passed between them until they reached the summit of the range and sat down on the cliff overhanging the sea.

This cliff was one of the numerous headlands which thrust their peaks in almost perpendicular lines sheer into the ocean.

They sat for an hour and drank in the peace and solemn grandeur of the infinite blue expanse.

"What a little world, the one in which we live down there and fret and fume," he whispered. "The one we think so big when in the thick of the fight! We forget the dim expanse of ocean kissing ocean — encircling the earth — of the skies that kiss the sea and lead on and on into those great silent deeps where a universe of worlds roll in grandeur!"

"Yet is n't man greater than all these worlds?" she asked, with sudden elation.

"If he is a man, yes: a real man with the con-

scious divine power in his soul which says, I
will! Is n't that the only power worth having?
The herd of cattle we call men, whose souls
have never spoken that divine word of character
and of action — are they men? Have they
souls at all? Is it worth the while of those who
have to fret and fuss and fume trying to make
something out of nothing?"

Barbara turned suddenly, looked into Norman's
eyes, and asked in anxious tones:

"What do you mean?"

"That I 'm thinking of giving up this
experiment."

"Now that you are just making it a marvellous
success?"

"But is it a success? What is the good of
achievement for any community if that achievement springs from the will of one man? If their
souls are in subjection to his, has he not degraded
them? Is life inside or outside? Are we
Socialists not struggling merely with what is
outside? Are we not in reality struggling back
into the primitive savage herd out of which
individual manhood has slowly emerged? I 'm
puzzled. I 'm afraid to go on. I 've asked you
to come up here to-day to tell me what to do."

Barbara's breath came quick.

"You wish me to decide the momentous

question of our colony? Perhaps the future of humanity?"

"Yes, just that. You are a woman. Women know things by intuition rather than by reason. I'm growing more and more to believe that we only know what we feel. I trust you as I would not trust my own judgment just now. I'm going to ask you, in the purity and beauty of your woman's soul, to read the future for me. I'm going to allow you to decide this question. Feel with me its difficulties and its prospects, trust utterly to your own intuitions, and you will decide right."

Barbara began to tremble and her voice was very low as she bent toward him.

"Why do you trust me with the greatest question of your life with such perfect faith?"

He took her hand, bowed, and kissed it.

"Because, Barbara, I love you," he whispered with passionate tenderness.

The girl looked away and smiled while her heart beat in an ecstasy of triumph.

"And this is one of the things that has puzzled me most," he went on, rapidly. "Every hope and dream my soul has cherished of you has been at war with this scheme of herding men and women together. I want you all my very own. I want to seize you now in my arms and carry

you a thousand miles away from every vulgar
crowd on earth. A hundred times I've been
on the point of telling you that I love you, but
I drew back and sealed my lips. It was treason
to the Cause. For how can this cause of the
herd be one with the heart-cry of the man for the
one woman on earth his mate? I've tried to
reconcile them, but I can't. Come, dearest, you
are my nobler, better self, the part of me I've been
searching for and have found. You must answer
this cry for light and guidance. Your voice shall
be to me the voice of God. Shall I go back to
the faith of my fathers in the old world, and
will you come with me — my wife, my mate,
my life? Or shall we remain here, and hand
in hand fight this battle to a finish? The one
thing that is unthinkable is that I shall lose
you. I lay my life at your feet. Do with it as
you will."

Barbara tried to speak and a sob choked her
into silence. She lifted her head at last and
spoke timidly.

"I thought it would be easy. But I find it
very, very difficult — this settling the destiny of
a man. Of one thing I'm sure. You must
not give up this work."

"I'll sign the deeds of transfer to-morrow,"
he interrupted.

The girl's eyes opened in wonder and a feeling of awe stole into her heart.

"You trust me so far?" she asked, brokenly.

"Yes."

"Then I must speak softly, must I not? I must weigh every word. You frighten me ——"

"I'm not afraid. You are the woman I love."

"How long have you loved me?" she asked, studying him curiously.

"Always, I think. Consciously since the day I tore that flag down on our lawn."

"And yet you drew away from me at times."

"Yes. I felt the irrepressible conflict between this ideal and my desires. Your voice called me to the work. I determined to put the work to the test first ——"

"And I was the inspiration behind your faith and daring leadership?"

"Always."

"You haven't asked me if I love you?" Barbara said, after a pause.

"I've been afraid."

"Why?"

"Because I don't think you are yet conscious of the meaning of love."

"And yet you place yourself absolutely in my power?"

"Absolutely. I love you and I have not made a mistake."

"Frankly, then, I don't know what love means. In my heart of hearts I've always been afraid of men ——"

"You're not afraid of me?"

"After to-day — no, I don't think I will be."

"You have made me very happy," he cried joyously. "Come, we must hurry back now. I'm going to make out the deeds to-night and place them in your hands to-morrow morning."

Scarcely a word was spoken as they descended the mountain. She had gone up in the morning a laughing girl, conscious of her beauty and its cruel power, and determined to use it. She came down a sober little woman with a great, wondering question growing in her heart.

When Wolf met her with eager questions she answered as in a dream.

"He will deliver the deeds to-morrow?" he gasped in amazement.

"Yes, to-morrow," she answered mechanically.

CHAPTER XXVII

THE FRUITS OF PATIENCE

THE next morning Norman asked Barbara to take breakfast alone with him in the little rose bower on the lawn where she had first announced her choice of work so oddly and charmingly.

She entered with a timid hesitation and a half-frightened look he was was quick to note. He was sure from the expression of her eyes that she had not slept.

"You did not sleep well?" he asked.

"I did n't sleep at all," she confessed.

"He attempted to take her hand and she drew back trembling.

"Now, you *are* afraid of me?"

"Yes. I 'm afraid I am," she stammered.

"Why of me? The one man of all men on earth — the man who loves you?"

"Perhaps that 's just why I 'm afraid of you," she said, with an effort to smile. "But, to tell you the truth, I think it 's just because you are a man. Last night I lay awake thinking it all over. I 'm quite sure that I shall always be afraid of men. I like you better than any man I 've ever known, but now that you 've told me you love me I 'm uneasy when I 'm near you. I think you 'd better give me up at once. I 'm sure I 'm hopeless as a sweetheart. I know I could never marry. The domestic instinct seems utterly missing in my nature. I love man in the abstract, but I can never surrender to any particular man. It seems like suicide. I want to be myself. I hate the idea of losing myself in another's being — I can't endure it, and if you make love to me any more I shall be very unhappy — and — I 'll have to keep out of your way. You won't do this any more will you? Promise me, and we will be our old selves again — just comrades."

Norman bowed with a smile.

"I promise never to speak another word of love to you until you tell me that you love me!"

"Honestly?" she laughed.

"On my word of honour," he answered, gravely.

"Then I shall be happy again," she cried.

"You will not try to avoid me?"

"No."

"You will help and cheer me in the work I 've planned?"

"Every day," she promised.

"Then I shall bide my time." He drew the

deeds to the island from his pocket and handed them to her.

"The title to a kingdom which I joyfully deliver by order of the queen-regent!"

"You are sure you do this because I asked you?"

"Do you really doubt it?"

"No," was the candid reply. "And I'll be frank enough to confess that I feel very proud of my power. You flattered my vanity as never before. You have put me under a sense of gratitude for which I fear I can never reward you."

"I have my reward in your approval."

She smiled and lifted her finger in warning.

"I'll not forget my promise," he said. "From to-day we understand each other perfectly. I am permitted to love you in silence. You graciously permit this as long as I am silent. In my wounded pride I have vowed that you yourself shall break this silence or it shall remain unbroken forever. This is our compact?"

"Yes," she answered extending her hand. He felt it tremble at his first touch and then rest contentedly and confidently in his strong grasp for a moment before they parted.

When once his decision was made, Norman threw every doubt to the winds and devoted himself with tireless zeal to establishing the

Brotherhood on the vast scale he had originally planned.

In every step of the expanding life of the colony Barbara was his constant companion and silent inspiration.

The transfer of the property was duly made under Wolf's keen gray eyes, with every detail of the law carefully guarded.

A second colony of two thousand enthusiasts was landed and established in the new building. Under Norman's inspiring leadership their work was quickly organized.

A new central administrative colony of five thousand was planned, and the foundation of its buildings laid with inspiring ceremonies. The huge structure was formed in the shape of a quadrangle covering ten acres of ground. In the centre of the court rose the house of the regents, in reality a palace of imposing splendour. The assembly hall was located in the regents' palace and formed the dining-room of their colony. At one end of the magnificent room was placed on an elevated platform the table at which the board of governors would sit, while at each end of the table stood the gilded chairs of state to be occupied by the regent and his consort.

The scheme of imposing grandeur was suggested by Wolf. Norman objected at first, but yielded at last, convinced by his past experiences that a central authority of undisputed power was essential to the existence of any state founded on the socialistic ideal.

At each corner of the quadrangle a public building was placed connected by the dormitories; on one corner was placed a theatre, on another a music hall, on another a school and nursery, on the other a lyceum to be used for public gatherings of all kinds, religious, social, or political. Each section of the outer buildings was connected with the regent's palace in the centre of the court by covered walk ways.

The entire force of the four thousand members of the Brotherhood (except the farmers) were placed at work to complete this structure at the earliest possible moment.

A day before the annual meeting of the Brotherhood at which the board of governors and the two regents were to be elected for the term of four years, Norman established a daily newspaper, *The New Era*, and the event was celebrated in the evening by a banquet and ball.

As he walked among the joyous throngs of the Brotherhood as they moved through the brilliantly lighted ball-room he began to feel for the first time the conscious joy of a great achievement.

Beyond a doubt the Brotherhood was an accomplished fact. Its fame was stirring the world beyond their little island. Pictures of the future flashed through his imagination, and always in greater and more alluring splendour.

He saw himself becoming more and more the guiding spirit of the great enterprise. If men opposed his plans he would mould their wills in his.

Gradually he meant to remove the hard and painful elements of force on which the efficiency of the colony now rested. The discipline of an army with its stern laws of physical violence back of its clock-like precision was not to his liking. He winced at the thought of that grim relic of barbarism, the whipping-post, which they had found necessary to temporarily revive. The jail, guardhouse, and penal colony were thorns in his flesh which he would remove at the earliest possible moment. The one excuse for their existence was the inheritance of evil in man's nature due to his wrongs and suffering under the system of capitalism. They would outgrow them.

Again and again he encountered Wolf and Catherine in the highest spirits, laughing, joking, chatting, shaking hands with each one they met.

Suddenly it struck him for the first time that he had a poor memory for names and faces. He wondered how Wolf could remember the name of the most obscure member of the colony without an effort. He had been so absorbed in the big problems of the Brotherhood that he had given little or no time to cultivating the personal acquaintance of its individual members. The arts of the politician were foreign to his nature. He had never stooped in his thoughts even to consider them. He had always lived in a different world.

Never for a moment had the idea occurred to him that he might have to fight for his position as leader of the colony which he had created, yet when he took his seat beside Barbara the following night to preside over the annual meeting, he was conscious instantly that through the crowd of eager faces before him there ran a strong current of personal hostility.

It was a disagreeable surprise. But as he recalled the many unpopular decisions he had been called on to make during the past year it seemed but natural there should be a lingering soreness in some minds. It was not until he saw Wolf in deep consultation with Diggs's glasses, and Catherine whispering to the smooth, gray-haired woman who had demanded the expulsion of Blanche, that he knew an organized plot had been formed to depose him from power.

His first impulse was one of blind rage. He recalled now with lightning flashes of memory the

long hours Wolf and his wife had spent in soothing
the anger of rebellious and troublesome members.
At every public meeting he recalled their smiling
faces at the door or moving through the hall.
The whole scheme was plain, its low chicanery,
its shallow hypocrisy, its fawning acceptance of
his leadership! They had been patiently waiting
for him to finish the work of strong, legal,
invincible, powerful organization to step in and
take the reins from his hands.

And they had done it with such consummate
skill, such infinite care and patience, that not one
of his own personal followers had discovered the
plot.

When the smooth, gray-haired woman rose to
nominate candidates for regent he knew, before
she spoke, the names she would pronounce. He
looked at her with a feeling of contempt and to
save his life he could n't recall her name.

She repeated her address to the chair with angry
emphasis:

"Comrade Chairman!"

"I beg your pardon," Norman answered,
"but I could not for the moment recall your name.
The comrade on my right (the woman without a
soul, he added in low tones) has the floor."

Barbara started at his tone of anger and
whispered:

"How could you be so rude — what is wrong ?"

"We are about to retire from office."

"What!" Barbara gasped as the little woman began to speak.

"Listen — you will understand," he said, with a sudden curve of his lip.

"Comrades," the deep, calm voice began, "I place in nomination for the office of regents for the four ensuing years the names of a man and woman whom every member of the old colony entitled to vote to-night has learned to love and honour—a man and woman whose ripe experience, whose sound judgment, whose sense of right, whose powers of reasoning, whose executive genius will give to us all the guarantee of perfect justice and perfect order ——"

"You bet they will, old girl," Tom cried with enthusiasm, waving his hand admiringly toward Norman and Barbara.

The speaker paused, regarded Tom a moment with quiet scorn, and continued:

"I have the honour to name for the highest honour in the gift of the Brotherhood for the regency of the new State of Ventura Comrades Herman and Catherine Wolf."

"What 's that you say ?" old Tom yelled with anger, leaping to his feet, and glaring around the room in a dazed surprise.

The old miner was too shrewd a politician to doubt now for a moment the situation. He made the only possible attack on the programme that promised results.

"In view of the fact, feller comrades," he shouted, "that half the present members er this here Brotherhood have not been here long enough to vote, I move that in justice to the new members we postpone this election for six months."

Joe seconded the motion, and the chairman asked:

"Are there any remarks on the motion?"

The Bard moved as if to rise, when Diggs snatched him back into his seat.

Amid a silence that was ominous the chairman put the question:

"All in favour of postponing this election for six months that our new members may be able to vote will say 'Aye.'"

The response was feeble. Tom and Joe yelled very loudly, but their effort was obvious.

"All in favour say 'No.'"

The whole audience seemed to shout in solid trained chorus "No!"

Tom hastened to nominate Norman and Barbara. The old miner's speech was couched in plain, uncouth words, but they came from the heart and their rugged eloquence stirred the crowd with surprising power. Diggs glanced over the audience through his flashing glasses, and his perpetual smile faded into a look of uneasiness as a round of applause swept the house.

He tiptoed to Wolf's side and whispered:

"Any danger?"

"Not the slightest. I want him to get some votes. It's better so."

The programme went through without a hitch. Wolf and Catherine were elected regents by an overwhelming majority and a new board of governors chosen with not a single one whom Norman knew personally.

The young leader sat in sullen silence, and watched the proceedings with contempt. Barbara looked on in increasing wonder and pain.

When the result was announced and the cheering had died away she bent her beautiful head close to his and whispered:

"This is a complete surprise. You believe me?"

"Yes," he quickly answered, "and one touch of your hand will rob defeat of its sting."

She pressed his hand with lingering tenderness and sought Catherine with a flash of anger in her brown eyes that boded trouble for the house of Wolf.

CHAPTER XXVIII

THE NEW MASTER

WOLF lost no time in demonstrating that he was complete master of the situation.

At nine o'clock next morning two armed guards, whom he had never seen in the house before, entered Norman's room and handed him the first official order of the new regents. The deposed young leader read it with amusement at first, but as his eyes rested on its brief words of command, something of their sinister meaning began to dawn in his mind.

"All citizens of the State of Ventura are ordered to immediately surrender their arms. By order of
"HERMAN WOLF,
"*Regent.*"

Norman looked at the revolvers in the holsters of the guards and dryly remarked:

"But the State will kindly continue their use, I see!"

Norman surrendered his revolver, and his room was searched in every nook and corner for weapons he might have concealed.

"Why this insult?" he demanded.

The guardsman saluted.

"Special orders of the regent, sir. We are to take no man's word for it."

Norman sat in silence while the men opened his trunks, ransacked his drawers, and searched in every conceivable spot where a weapon of any kind might be hid.

"I could have told you at first that I had no other guns . The entire colony is being disarmed this morning?"

"Yes, sir, the work will be completed by two o'clock."

"Indeed!"

The man fumbled in his pocket and drew out another order.

"And this one for you personally, sir."

"Oh — after the disarming?"

"Yes, sir!"

Norman read the second order and the lines of his mouth tightened suddenly. The note was brief but to the point:

"Comrade Norman Worth will report to the regent at ten o'clock for orders.

"HERMAN WOLF,
"*Regent.*"

For five minutes after the guards had gone Norman stood in silence staring at this order.

It was the first he had ever received in his life except the one from his own father which he had disobeyed.

To be driven into another man's presence to take orders as from a master to a servant was an idea that had never entered his imagination. He had seen such things. He had given orders, but he had never, somehow, counted himself in the class of men who took them.

For the first time he began to realize the meaning of the work he had been doing, and began to see how deftly and unconsciously he had been forging the chains of a system of irresponsible slavery on his fellow men. While the motive which impelled him was one of unselfish love, and he had thought only of their best interest, he saw now in a flash with what crushing cruelty this power could be used.

It all seemed simple enough when he regarded his own will as the centre and source of power. Now that another man had grasped the lever and applied this power, the whole scheme of artificial life which he had created took on a new and darker meaning.

What should he do?

His first impulse was to walk into Wolf's presence, denounce him as a scheming scoundrel, and defy his power. That Wolf would fight was not to be questioned for a minute. His first act of disarming the colony was a master-stroke, and the longer the young leader thought of it the more hopeless his present situation became.

Beyond a doubt Wolf had been selecting the new regent's guard with the same patience and skill with which he had executed his political coup. This guard was composed now only of his tried and trusted henchmen. A single false step on Norman's part would simply play into the wily brute's hands, and he would destroy himself at a single stroke.

He must use his brain. He must fight the devil with fire. He must submit for the moment, plan and work and wait with infinite patience, and when the work of patience was complete, then strike and strike to kill.

And yet the blood rushed to his heart and strangled with the thought of submission to such a man. But there was no other way. He had himself set the trap of steel he now felt crash into his own flesh.

To appeal to his father was unthinkable — his pride forbade it, even if it were possible.

To escape was out of the question. Every way had been cut and that by his own order. The mail was inspected. The steamer held no communication with the people of the island.

No boat was allowed to land, and no boat, even the smallest sail or row boat, was permitted to a member of the Brotherhood on any pretext.

Besides, resignation or flight could not be thought of for another reason. To retreat now and leave thousands of people behind whom he had led into this enterprise would be the act of a coward.

There was nothing left except to fight it out on the lines he had himself laid down.

The one thing that hurt him most was the ugly suspicion that Barbara must have known something of this deeply laid scheme by which the Wolfs had gained control of the Brotherhood. And yet her surprise had been genuine, her anger real. He could n't be mistaken about it. To believe her capable of such treachery and double-dealing was to doubt the very existence of truth and purity.

And yet, when he recalled how little he really knew of her past life, what dark secrets might lurk in the story of the years she had spent under the same roof with these people, he grew sick at the thought.

He knew now that the blond beast with the red scar on his neck and the slender, dark-eyed madonna-like mate who had always been his shadow were capable of anything. Two people who could smile in treacherous silence for a year and suddenly grip the throat of the man who had been their best friend, needed no written biography to tell their past. It was luminous. And in the glare in which he read it he shuddered at the sinister light it threw on the beautiful girl whom they had reared as their own.

He took from his mantel a little picture made one day in San Francisco by a tintype man. It was a singularly beautiful likeness of Barbara, taken on a sudden impulse without a moment's thought or preparation. Her laughing face looked out at him, wreathed in a garland of wayward ringlets of dark brown hair. Truth, sincerity, beauty, intelligence, and a childlike innocence were stamped in every line.

A thousand times since he had seen her just like that. And from the moment of their advent on the island this impression of girlish innocence and sincerity had grown rather than decreased. The more he saw of her in the simpler, quieter moments of their association, the stronger, deeper, and more tender his love became, and the deeper grew his utter faith in the purity of her soul and body.

"I'll sooner doubt an angel of God!" he said at last, as he placed it back on the mantel.

He would see Wolf at once, learn his plans, and then carefully make his own.

He dressed with care and at the appointed hour rapped for admission at the executive office where the day before he sat as master.

He was told the regent was busy with others and ordered to wait his turn. He flushed with anger, recovered himself, waited a half hour, and was ushered into the presence of the new ruler.

Wolf sat in the big revolving chair at his desk with conscious dignity and power. Two of his guards stood outside the door, grim reminders of the substantial character of the new administration.

Norman seated himself with careless ease without invitation and waited for the older man to speak.

Wolf smiled grimly, stroked his thick, coarse reddish beard, and looked at Norman thoughtfully a moment.

"Well, my boy," the regent began, with friendly patronage, "we'd as well come to the point without ceremony. You are down and out. The new board of governors will do what I wish. I am in supreme command of the ship of state. Do you want to fight or work?"

"It's a poor doctor, Wolf," Norman said, coolly, "who can't take his own medicine. I came here to work."

"Congratulations on your good sense!" the regent replied. "I've no desire to make trouble for you. I have nothing against you personally. I had to put you out and take command to save the colony from ruin. You meant well, but you were a bungling amateur, and you can be of greater service in the ranks than in command. I know you don't like me after what has happened, but you don't have to. I'll be generous. What sort of work would you like to have assigned you?"

"Thanks, that's very kind of you, Wolf, I'm sure. I believe the warden of every penitentiary is equally generous to all convicts. However, that's a minor detail, seeing that I assisted in the creation of this ideal world."

Wolf smashed the desk top with his big fist and suddenly glared at Norman, his cold eyes gleaming angrily.

"Come to the point! I've no time to waste! Have you any choice as to the kind of work to which you wish to be assigned?"

"I have a decided choice. Our mines have all failed. I'll redeem the failure by perfecting and completing the big dredge for mining gold from the low-grade sands on the beach."

"A waste of time and money," Wolf snapped. "I can't afford to spare the men on any more fool inventions. Such things must stop."

"You mean to stop all progress by stopping inventions?" Norman asked.

"So far as the State is concerned, yes," said the regent, with emphasis. "Under your slipshod administration we spent nearly two hundred thousand dollars during the past year on so-called inventions. Every fool in the colony has invented something. Not one in a hundred has produced an idea that is practicable. We cannot afford to waste the capital of the State in such idiocy."

"Give me twenty men and I'll complete the dredge."

"Labour is capital in the Socialist State. I can't afford to waste it."

"But you are not wasting it," Norman pleaded. "I've spent sixty thousand already on this invention. Unless the machine is completed the capital will be lost to the colony."

"It will be lost anyhow," Wolf answered, impatiently. "Your whole conception is a piece of childish folly. You can't make a profit operating a dredge in sand containing only twenty cents' worth of gold to a ton of dirt."

"I can do better," Norman urged with enthusiasm. "I can make a hundred per cent. on the investment if the dirt pans out ten cents to the ton. If it pans twenty cents a ton I can make millions."

"So every crank has claimed for his particular piece of idiocy. I'll not permit another dollar or another day's labour to be thrown away on any such crazy experiment."

Norman's face reddened with a rush of uncontrollable anger.

"Look here, Wolf, you can't be serious in this."

"I was never more serious in my life," the big jaws snapped. "I am going to issue an order to-day that hereafter any man or woman who conceives an invention can work it out himself without aid from the State. They must do this at odd hours after working the required time each day. They must put their own money into their machine."

"As the State only has capital," Norman protested, "this means the practical prohibition of all invention. No man can with his own hands make the machinery needed in the progress of humanity. We have abolished private capital by abolishing rent, interest, and profit. Do you propose thus to stop the progress of the world?"

"No," Wolf cried with a wave of his heavy hand. "Let the ambitious inventor work at night and build his own machine. I will grant, in my order on the subject, to each successful inventor the right to operate his own machine for ten years before it becomes the property of the State."

"Suppose he succeeds," said Norman, "under such hard conditions with his own hands and without capital in perfecting an invention of enormous value, such as the dredge I have begun, of what use will the results be if he cannot invest them in rent or interest, and all gifts and exchanges are prohibited?"

"He may build a home and lavish them on his wife and children, or he may become a great public benefactor and win the love and gratitude of the people by enriching the State and shortening the hours of labour. If your dredge can make a million, for example, as you claim—go ahead, work at night, perfect it, put it to work, build yourself a palace to live in, give millions to the Brotherhood. Shorten their hours from eight to four, and I 'll guarantee you 'll oust me from my position of power."

Norman's eye suddenly flashed with resolution.

"You will not grant me the labour to complete the dredge?" Norman asked.

"Not one man for one minute," was the curt reply.

"Then I 'll finish it myself," Norman said, with determination.

"After you 've worked eight full hours a day, under my direction — you understand!" the regent responded sullenly.

Norman sprang to his feet and the two men faced each other a moment, the big scar on Wolf's neck flashing red, his enormous fists instinctively closing.

"Wolf, this is an infamous outrage!"

"I'll teach you not to speak to me in that manner again, sir!" the regent slowly said, as he tapped his bell.

The guards sprang to his side.

"Show this gentleman to the barnyard — he is a good farmer. Put him at work with old Methodist John cleaning out the stables for the new cantaloup crop. He is very fond of cantaloups. If he makes any trouble tell the sergeant of your guard to give him thirty-nine lashes without consulting me."

Norman stepped closer, and, trembling from head to foot, said to Wolf:

"If ever one of your men lays the weight of his hand on me ——"

"And yet we both agreed that under our system discipline must be enforced — the discipline of an army?" the regent interrupted.

Norman held his gaze fixed without moving a muscle, and slowly continued:

"If you ever try it, you'd better finish your job."

"I'll remember your advice," Wolf answered with a sneer. "Show him to his work."

CHAPTER XXIX

A TEST OF STRENGTH

WHEN Catherine saw the furious look on Barbara's face as she descended from the platform the night of the election, she avoided a meeting and went to bed pleading a headache.

Early the next morning Barbara rapped for entrance, forced her way in, and stood, tense with anger, before the older woman, her eyes red from the long vigil of a sleepless night.

"You avoided me last night ——"

Catherine laughed.

"My dear, I never saw you in quite such a rage. It might be serious if it were not so silly."

"You 'll find it serious before you are through with this performance," Barbara retorted, angrily.

"Remember, I am in supreme authority now. Don't you dare speak to me in that manner, you ungrateful little wretch!"

"I 'll dare to tell you the truth — even if you were the mother who bore me — even if I had not repaid you a hundredfold for every dollar you have spent on me."

"Hush, hush, my dear, I do not wish to quarrel," Catherine said, recovering herself. "I know your pride is wounded over your defeat. I 've watched your growing vanity in high office with much amusement for the past year."

"I 'm not thinking of myself," Barbara said with emphasis.

"Of course not — what woman ever does ?" Catherine sneered.

"I am glad to be relieved of the annoyance of such a position. But your treatment of the brave and daring young spirit who conceived this colony and created its wealth and influence ——"

"Am I responsible ?"

"Yes. Herman is incapable of conceiving such a plot without your suggestion. It is your work. You have always loved luxury and power."

"Perhaps I love a man also," Catherine interrupted, as her full sensuous lips curled in a curious smile.

"Yes, I give you credit for that too," the girl admitted. "Though I confess the secret of your infatuation for that hulking brute has always been one of the black mysteries of life to me."

"When you 're older," again the round lips quivered with a smile, "perhaps you will understand. And now, my child, I 've been patient with you. But don't you ever again call Herman a brute in my presence."

"Take care he does n't prove it to you!" the girl warned.

Catherine suddenly paled.

"What do you mean by that?" she whispered, glancing about the room.

"Nothing! nothing! nothing! Only that in every deed of the devil there is the seed of death. You have planted the seed. The harvest is sure."

"My dear ——"

"Don't call me that again! I hate you!" Barbara spoke with deliberate passion.

"Have you gone mad?" Catherine cried, with impatience.

"Yes, mad with hatred. From to-day we are enemies, and I 'll hate you forever!"

The older woman looked at her in astonishment and spoke with a deliberate sneer:

"As you like. Remember, then, from this moment that you are a servant under my command. I am no longer your foster-mother. Leave this room instantly, take your things to the domestic servants' quarters, and report to the head-woman for duty in the corridors of this wing of the building."

"And you think I 'll submit to this?" Barbara gasped.

Catherine rang the bell, and Barbara gazed at her with a look of mingled terror and rage. A sudden light flashed in her brown eyes.

"You mean this?"

"I'll show you in a moment," was the calm reply.

"Then it's war between us," Barbara cried.

She sprang to the door and Catherine caught her arm.

"Where are you going?"

"To Herman."

"He cannot interfere with my decisions."

Barbara threw her off and bounded through the door crying:

"We shall see!"

The girl rushed past the guard at the door of Wolf's office, trembling with rage, her eyes filled with blinding tears.

Wolf sprang to his feet in astonishment and met her with outstretched hands.

"What's the matter, child?" he asked as his big coarse fists closed over the hot little fingers and his gray eyes lighted at the sight of her dishevelled hair and bare throat.

Barbara choked back the sobs, and looked appealingly into Wolf's face.

"We have quarrelled about last night. You understand, Herman. Catherine has ordered me to leave my room and join the servants in the halls. You — you will not allow me to be degraded thus — will you?"

Wolf drew the trembling girl into his arms, pressed her close a moment, stroked her curls with his gnarled hand, and his face flushed with a look of triumph.

"Don't worry, dear, I'll protect you," he answered, bending and kissing her forehead. "Go back to your room, and if any one dares to disturb you, call for me."

Barbara murmured through her tears:

"Thank you, Herman."

Wolf's eyes sparkled as he watched the graceful little figure proudly leave the room.

CHAPTER XXX

A VISION FROM THE HILLTOP

CATHERINE'S fight with Wolf was long and bitter. For hours she struggled to force him to leave in her hands the discipline of the women members of the colony. Her tears and threats fell on ears equally deaf to all pleading. At last the guards listening outside heard only the low sobbing of a woman's voice near the door for a half hour without a sound from the man.

And then his short, sharp words came quick and curt and stinging:

"Are you done now with this fool performance?"

The answer was a sob.

"Understand once for all," the cold, hard voice went on, "I am the master here. Your office as regent is one of courtesy only as my wife. My word alone is supreme. When you cease to be my wife another regent will be chosen and I do the choosing. I not only propose to do the work of disciplining the women, but it is the one kind of work to which I shall devote myself with pleasure."

"Herman!" Catherine sobbed, as if she had sunk beneath a blow.

The man laughed with brutal enjoyment.

"You 'd as well know this now as later. You can be getting used to it."

Her eyes red with weeping, her proud shoulders drooped for the first time in her life, Catherine slowly walked from Wolf's office back to her room.

Barbara passed her on the stairs without a word or a glance, and hurried again to see the regent, her whole being alert with quick intelligence.

The guard had received instructions that she was the one privileged person in the colony who could enter his office at all hours, day or night, without ceremony or delay. They showed her in immediately.

"I 've just heard of your order sending Norman to the work of a common farm-hand, Herman," Barbara began.

Wolf scowled.

"You must not interfere in this little affair between my rival and myself, Barbara," he said, sternly.

"I will interfere," she quickly replied, "both for your sake and his. You 've made a serious mistake, Herman. Correct it at once."

"I had to show him his place."

"It is n't fair. The men will resent it. You will make enemies. Your power is complete. You can afford to be generous."

Wolf looked at her with hungry, admiring gaze."

"Perhaps you 're right," he said slowly.

"Of course I 'm right!" she replied, "and you know it. You 've made him a martyr and a hero on the first day of his fall from power. Your true policy is just the opposite. Let him do what he pleases for a time. Above all things don't put yourself in the position of his enemy. Your strength lies in standing as his patron and friend."

"By Jove, Barbara," Wolf cried, "what a wise head on your little shoulders! Come, be honest with me now — you 're not in love with this man ?"

The girl smiled demurely:

"He is with me, I think," she admitted.

"Yes, yes, of course — so we all are," he cried, with a smile. "But you have not accepted his love ?"

"No."

"I thought you had better sense. I 'll change my order at your suggestion."

"I knew you would," she cried, joyfully.

Wolf sat down at his desk and wrote:

"Comrade Norman Worth is transferred from the field to the foundry, with permission, after his day's work, to employ his time in the shops perfecting any invention in which he may be interested.

"WOLF — *Regent.*"

He handed the order to Barbara.

"Take this to the youngster and tell him I did it at your suggestion, and hereafter give him a wide berth if you wish to be friendly with me."

Barbara dropped her eyes and Wolf touched her chin with his coarse, short fingers.

"A hint to the wise is sufficient, little girl. You understand?"

Barbara took the order, turned toward the door, paused and smiled coquettishly:

"I understand, Herman."

She found Norman at work with Methodist John cleaning out a stable. To her amazement he was whistling and joking about something with the old man. She stopped and listened a moment.

"But what on earth do you want a lightning-rod for, John?" Norman asked.

"That's my secret, sir," the old man answered, "but I must have one — won't you get it for me?"

"I'm sorry, John, but I have no more power now in the State of Ventura than you have."

"But did n't you get the million dollars and did n't you make all the money for 'em — a hundred and fifty thousand dollars on the cantaloups the others did n't have sense enough to plant? Surely they 'll give you enough to get me a thirty-foot lightning-rod?"

"I 'm afraid not, John, still I 'll do my best. I don't like to press you for the secrets of your inner life, old man, but I 've immense curiosity to know what you want with that lightning-rod? You say you 're not afraid of lightning?"

"No, sir, I 'm not afraid of nothin'."

"Then why ——"

"'T ain't no use in askin' sir, I can't tell ye. But I want it. I 'm going to pray every night for it till I get it. Maybe the Lord will send me one by an angel ——"

Barbara suddenly appeared in the door of the stall.

"Speaking of angels," Norman cried, laughing.

"I have an order for you," Barbara said, quickly.

Norman threw his pitchfork full of manure out of the window of the stall, stood the fork in the corner, brushed his hands, and bowed before Barbara.

"What an exquisite picture you make standing in the doorway there with that ocean of blossoming peach trees stretching up the slope until it kisses the sky line. I wish I were an artist."

She looked at him with amazement.

"I expected to find you with murder in your heart. I can't understand."

Norman took the note from her white fingers.

"Because I 'm laughing?"

"Yes."

"Well, is n't the joke on me? I 've been preaching, preaching, preaching, about the dignity of all labour. I kicked the first few moments, I confess. The medicine was bitter, but I soon began to find that it was good for the soul. I 'm getting acquainted with myself ——"

Norman paused, read Wolf's order, and looked tenderly into Barbara's eyes.

"So you heard of my fall and came to my rescue. It 's worth the jolt to be rescued by such a hand."

He stooped and kissed the tips of her fingers.

"Come with me up the hill yonder among those blossoming trees," he said, leading her toward the orchard. "I want to tell you about a vision I saw in that stable a while ago while I wielded the pitchfork and talked to my old pauper friend, both of us now comrade equals."

They walked on in silence through the long, clean rows of fruit trees in full bloom, the air redolent with sweet perfume and quivering with the electric hum of growing life. On the top of the hill they paused and looked toward the sea that stretched away in solemn, infinite grandeur. Below, on the next plateau, rolled in apparently endless acres, the great white carpet of flowering plum trees and further on the tender budding grapes and beyond, lower still, the deep green valley with orange trees flashing their golden fruit.

"What a glorious world!" Barbara cried.

"Yes," he answered with a sigh, "a world of endless beauty in which after all there's nothing vile but man. And I once thought that in such a world angels only could live."

"Must we despair because one man or woman proves false," she asked.

"No," he answered cheerily, leading her to a boulder and taking his seat by her side.

"I don't despair. I've been seeing visions to-day — visions as old as the beat of the human heart, perhaps, yet always new."

He drew the order of Wolf from his pocket and looked at it.

"From the moment of my awakening last night from the fool's paradise in which I've been living the past year my mind has been at work on solving the one unsolved problem in this dredge to which he refers. It came to me like a flash while at work this morning."

"Your invention will succeed?" she interrupted.

"Beyond the shadow of a doubt," he said, with enthusiasm. "I did n't solve it before because I lacked the incentive to apply my mind to it."

"And you got the incentive in your defeat?" she asked, in surprise.

"Yes. Deprived of my toys, I came back to myself, the source of power."

"But your incentive — I don't understand — in such an hour?"

"A very simple, very old, but very powerful one, I 'm beginning to think, the source of all human progress—the determination to build a home here in one of these flower-robed hills overlooking the sea, and bring my bride to it some glorious day like this when every tree is festooned with joy! I don't want a modest cottage. My bride was born a queen. Every line of her delicate and sensitive face proclaims her royal ancestry. She shall have a palace. Love, Beauty, Music, Art, and Truth shall be her servants. I shall be the magician who will create all this out of the dirt men are now trampling under foot along the beach."

Barbara drew a deep breath, trembled, and looked away.

"I promised her never to speak of love again until her own dear lips called me, and I will not, though I fear sometimes the waiting seems long."

"And if she never calls?" the girl asked, dreamily.

"Then my palace shall remain silent and empty. Her hand alone can open its doors."

"And if I do not see you often while your palace is building, you may know at least I have not forgotten — and you will understand?"

"Yes, I will understand," he answered, with elation.

CHAPTER XXXI

IN LOVE AND WAR

WITH untiring zeal Norman gave himself to work on the dredge. Wolf refused to modify his original order that a full day should first be given as a labourer in the foundry and machine shops before he could devote himself to his invention.

This proved an advantage rather than a hindrance. By his unfailing courtesy, good fellowship, skill, and wit, Norman won his fellow workmen as warm personal friends. He was able thus to secure all the assistance he needed in his work.

Within two months the big dredge was finished.

From the first the regent had regarded Norman's fad with contempt. That he could succeed in making money out of dirt containing but twenty cents' worth of gold to a ton was an absurdity on its face.

While the young inventor worked day and night with tireless energy the regent quietly perfected his grip on the life of the rapidly growing colony. To render escape from the island or communication with the coast more impossible than ever, he established the strict system of double patrol around each community. No member of the Brotherhood was allowed to leave his room at night without permission. Beyond the outer patrol a mounted guard was established and the entire line of beach was guarded by watchmen in relays who reported each hour, day and night, by telephone to the commandant.

At the end of two months of Wolf's merciless rule the efficiency of labour had so decreased, it was necessary to lengthen the number of hours from eight to nine. As every inducement to efficiency of labour had been removed there was no incentive to any man to do more than he must without a fight with his guard or overseer. No vote was permitted on the question of increasing the hours of labour. The board of governors passed the order which Wolf wrote out for them without a dissenting voice.

Norman had no trouble in getting a gang of willing hands to push the monster gold-digger into position on one of the sand-points inside the harbour.

It was mounted on a float twenty-five feet wide and sixty-five feet long. For power it carried two fifty-horse-power distillate engines. Tom was in charge of one and Joe of the other. For raising the sand and gravel containing the gold two big Jackson gravel-pumps were located on opposite corners at the front end of the float.

Old Tom blew the whistle, the engines started, and in an hour the pumps had raised a hundred tons of sand and gravel and deposited them in the concentrating flumes. Norman worked the dredge all night without a moment's pause and in twelve hours his pumps had lifted fifteen hundred tons of sand, showing a capacity of 3,000 tons per day. When the gold was extracted and weighed it was found that the dredge had averaged twenty cents from each ton of sand and that it would cost less than three cents a ton to operate the entire machinery of its production. The first experimental machine alone would net $500 dollars a day, or $150,000 a year. He could put five of these machines to work in three months and make $3,000 a day.

The invention stirred the colony to its depths. Norman's appearance was the signal for a burst of cheering wherever he went.

Wolf was dumfounded. He called his board of governors together at once and ordered them to enact a new law to meet the situation.

Norman announced in the *Era* that he would give the Brotherhood from the beginning one half the net earnings of his machines, and asked the board of governors at once to grant him the men needed to build and operate enough dredges to reduce the hours of labour from nine to seven.

Wolf met the emergency with prompt and vigorous action. He suspended the editor for printing the announcement and set him to work carrying a hod.

He issued a proclamation as regent that the dredge in the hands of its inventor threatened the existence of the State, declared the law of inventions under which it was built suspended, and ordered Norman to at once operate the machine for the sole benefit of the State and begin the construction of twenty dredges of equal capacity.

When Norman received this order he set to work without a moment's delay and made a half-dozen dynamite bombs, gave one each to Tom and Joe and their assistants, laid in a supply of provisions, erected a tent on the beach beside the dredge, and set the big machine to work for all it was worth.

Wolf promptly ordered his arrest. The men who attempted to execute the order fled in terror at the sight of the bombs and reported for instructions.

Wolf came in person at the head of a picked company of fifty guards.

Norman had stretched a rope a hundred feet from the dredge and posted a notice that he would kill any man daring to cross it without his permission.

Wolf paused at the rope. Norman stood alone on one of the big pumps with his arms folded watching his enemy in silence.

The captain of the guard laid his hand on the regent's arm:

"You 'd better not try it."

"He won't dare," Wolf growled.

"Yes, he will," the captain insisted.

"I 'll risk it," the regent snapped.

"Are you mad? What's the use? He 'll blow it up. You can't rebuild the dredge — no one understands it. Use common sense. Send the girl with a flag of truce and ask for a conference."

"A good idea — if it works," Wolf answered hesitating.

"It 's worth trying," the captain urged.

Wolf returned to the house with his men, and in a few minutes Barbara came to Norman, her face white with terror, her voice quivering with pleading intensity.

"Please," she gasped, "for my sake, I beg of you not to do this insane thing! The regent asks for a conference under a flag of truce. He recognizes that it is impossible that you should remain here after what has happened. He asks for a half-hour's talk with you to offer an adjustment under which you can resign and return to San Francisco."

"It's a trick and a lie. He's deceiving you," Norman replied, sullenly.

"No, I swear it's true. He is in earnest, Catherine is beside herself with fear lest he be killed. He swore to her as he swore to me to respect your wishes. I'll gladly give my life if he proves false."

Norman turned his face away and looked over the still, blue waters, struggling with himself as he felt the tug of her soft hand on his heart.

Suddenly a hundred men with Wolf at their head sprang over the steep embankment and rushed to the dredge. Tom leaped to his feet and lifted his bomb without a word.

Norman covered Barbara and grasped his uplifted arm.

"It's all over boys. I've surrendered!" he shouted.

Barbara faced Wolf with blazing eyes:

"You have betrayed my trust!"

Wolf brushed her aside and confronted Norman, who had thrown the bomb he had taken from Tom's hand into the sea.

Norman paid no attention to Wolf, and seemed

to see only the girl's face convulsed with passion. His eyes never left her for a moment.

Wolf turned and secured the other men who had defended the dredge, marching them with their hands tied behind their backs between two rows of guardsmen off to jail.

Norman spoke at last to Barbara in low, cold tones:

"I congratulate you."

"What do you mean?" she gasped.

"That you are a superb actress. You have played your part to perfection. Your rôle was very dramatic, too. A clumsy woman would have bungled it, and lost even at the last moment."

"You cannot believe that I willingly betrayed you?" she cried, in anguish.

"I wish I had died before I knew it," he answered, bitterly.

Barbara pressed close to his side and seized his hand fiercely. He turned away with a shudder.

"Look at me," she pleaded.

He turned and faced her with a look of anger.

"Words are idle. Deeds speak louder than words."

"Norman, you are killing me with this cruel doubt!" she sobbed. "I give up! I love you! I love you!"

She threw her arms around his neck and her head sank on his breast.

He resisted for a moment, then clasped her to his heart, bent and kissd her with passionate tenderness.

"You believe me now?" she cried, through her tears.

"God forgive me for doubting you for a moment!" he answered, earnestly.

The guard suddenly drew Norman from her arms, tied his hands, and led him away to prison while the little figure followed, sobbing in helpless anguish.

Wolf walked behind, his big mouth twitching with smiles he could not suppress.

CHAPTER XXXII

A PRIMITIVE LOVER

WOLF led Barbara into his office, lighted the lamp, and waited in patience for her first blinding surrender to grief to spend itself before speaking.

He stood over her at last with a smile, bent and touched her brown curls.

The girl sprang to her feet and faced him.

"It 's no use, my beauty, I 'm on to your tricks now!"

The little figure stiffened, and her gaze was steady, though her fingers trembled as she nervously twisted the tiny handkerchief she held.

"You 've been playing me for a fool for the past two months. Your eyes have been laughing into mine with all sorts of little daring suggestions when you had an axe to grind at my expense. And then you had a habit of disappearing until you needed something else. You were off billing and cooing with our hero and smiling at my stupidity behind my back."

"I 've spoken to him to-day," Barbara answered

solemnly, "the first words of love that ever passed my lips."

"You did pretty well for an amateur, if that was the first kiss you ever gave him."

"It was the first!" she said, defiantly.

"It will be the last for him."

"Perhaps," she answered, with a curl to her lips.

"You think I don't mean it?" Wolf demanded, stepping close and thrusting his massive head forward while his big fists closed.

"I don't doubt it," she answered, firmly. "But I'm not afraid of you, Herman."

"You doubt my power?" he asked.

"Over others, no."

"But over you?"

Wolf suddenly grasped her.

The girl shrank back in terror for an instant, and then, to his surprise, her hand was still and cold and steady. Not a tremor in the tense body. Her brown eyes, staring wide, held his gaze without a sign of weakness or of fear. Something in her attitude startled the beast within him. He suddenly dropped her hand and changed his tone.

"Come, let's not quarrel! Don't be foolish. It is for you I've been scheming and planning the past year. For you the regent's palace was planned. Within five years a hundred thousand

"Wolf Grasped Her."

people wili be here. The State will be rich beyond our wildest dreams, and I shall be the State. I want you to sit by my side."

"You say this to me after all that Catherine has been to you and your life?"

"And why not? If I no longer love, should I be chained?"

"And this is the ideal you came here to build?" she asked, with scorn.

"Certainly. It is the essence of Socialism. In my next proclamation I shall declare for the freedom of love. Every great Socialist has preached this. Marriage and the family form the taproot out of which the whole system of capitalism grew. The system can never be destroyed until the family is annihilated. I had thought you a woman whose brilliant intellect had faced this issue and broken the chains of a degrading bourgeois morality."

"The chains of love, I find, are very sweet," she interrupted, with dreamy tenderness.

"You talk this twaddle about romantic love? You, the leader of a revolution! Come, you are no longer a child. We are living now in the world of freedom and reality where men and women say the unspoken things and live to the utmost reach of their being, body and soul."

"Is it a world worth living in?" she asked.

"Was the old world of family life, of starvation and misery, worth living in?" Wolf retorted.

"Perhaps I might have said no an hour ago, but now that my lips have met my lover's the dream of the old family life, with its sanctity and purity, begins to call me. And something deep down within answers with a cry of joy. Why should you desire me, knowing that I thus love another?"

"You can love where you like," he snapped, as his big jaws came together. "I can get along without your love. I just want you — and I 'm going to have you!"

"I 'll die first!"

"We shall see. Time works wonders."

With a shudder Barbara turned and left him.

CHAPTER XXXIII

EQUALITY

BARBARA asked Wolf for permission to visit Norman in prison.

The Regent shook his head.

"No, my little beauty, it's not wise. I promise you that not a hair of his head shall be harmed. He is safe and well. If you wish to test my power, try to bribe my guards and see him."

Day after day Barbara sought in vain to gain admittance to the jail, send or receive a message from within. Her lover had disappeared as completely as if the earth had opened and swallowed his body.

The episode of the dredge was the last effort to question the power of the regent. The day after its capture Wolf put the men who had helped Norman build it to work operating the big machine, and its huge pumps began to throb in perfect time, piling ton on ton of gold-bearing sand and gravel into the flumes, as faithful to the touch of the thief who had stolen it as to the hand of the man of genius who invented it.

The head machinist he ordered to build

five duplicates, and placed the entire working force of the mechanical department at once on the job.

The daily *New Era* received a number of protests against the outrage of the inventor's arrest and imprisonment. Two protests were signed by the names of the writers, Diggs and the Bard. There appeared in the paper a warning editorial against sneaks who, under cover of the cause of justice, were seeking to aid treason and rebellion against the State.

Diggs and the Bard were summoned before Wolf in person.

The regent fixed his gray eyes on Diggs, and the man of questions forgot to smile.

"You are not dealing with an amateur now, Diggs," Wolf said, with a sneer. "The insulting letter you wrote ——"

"I — I — beg your pardon, Mr. Regent," Diggs stammered, "my questions were asked in the spirit of honest inquiry."

"I understand their spirit, sir," Wolf growled. "And don't you interrupt me again when I 'm talking! Your article was seditious. I 've a mind to imprison you a year, but as this is your first offence I 'll simply transfer you from the department of accounts to that of garbage and sewerage. Report at once to the overseer."

Diggs's lips quivered and he tried to speak, but Wolf froze him with a look and he dropped to a seat.

"I said report at once, sir, to the overseer of the department of garbage and sewerage. Did you hear me?" Wolf thundered.

Diggs leaped to his feet stammering and retreating.

"Yes, sir! Yes, sir! Excuse me. I was only waiting for Comrade Adair, sir! Excuse me, sir, I'll go at once!"

He stumbled through the door and disappeared.

The Bard of Ramcat watched this scene with increasing terror. He had prepared an eloquent and daring appeal for freedom of speech. He tried to open his mouth, but Wolf's gaze froze the blood in his veins. His tongue refused to move. He sat huddled in a heap, trembling and shifting uneasily in his seat.

At length the regent spoke with sneering patronage:

"You wield a facile pen, Adair. I admire the glib ability with which your pour out gaseous matter from your overheated imagination."

The Bard scrambled to his feet and bowed low in humble submission, fumbling his slouch hat tremblingly.

"I meant no harm, sir, I assure you. A great

leader of your power and genius can make allowances for poetic fervour. I 'm sure you know that my whole soul is aflame with enthusiasm for our noble Cause!''

"Well, upon my word," Wolf laughed, "you 're developing into a nimble liar! You used to be quite brutal in the frankness of your criticisms.''

"But I see the error of my way, sir," the Bard humbly cried.

"Then I 'll remit your prison sentence also and merely transfer you to the stone-quarry. We need more common labourers on the rock-pile there preparing the macadam for the court of the regent's palace. Report at once to the foreman of that gang.''

"Thank you, sir," the Bard stammered, feebly, as he backed out of the room.

The poet bent his proud back over the stone-pile for two weeks and suddenly disappeared.

His hat was found on a rustic seat on a high cliff whose perpendicular wall was washed by the sea. Beneath this hat lay his last manuscript protest to the world. It was entitled:

"The Journal of Roland Adair, Bard of Ramcat.'' It was written in blank verse and proved a most harrowing recital of the horrors he had suffered at the hands of the tyrant regent. With eloquence fierce and fiery he called on the slaves who were being ground beneath his heel to rise in their might and slay the oppressor. He had chosen to die that his death-song might stir their souls to heroic action.

Search was made on the beaches for his body in vain. His wife's grief was genuine and a few of his friends gathered with her on the tenth day after his disappearance to express their sorrow and appreciation in a brief formal service.

Diggs was delivering a funeral oration bombarding Death, Hell, and the Grave with endless questions, when suddenly the Bard appeared, pinched with hunger, his clothes covered with dirt, his long hair dishevelled and unkempt. He had evidently been sleeping in the open.

His friends stood in wonder. His wife shrieked in terror.

The Bard solemnly lifted his hand and cried:

"I stood on the hills and waited for slaves to rise and fight their way to death or freedom. And no man stirred! Did they not find my death-song?"

Diggs spoke in timid accents:

"The regent destroyed it."

"Yes, yes, but before my death I anticipated his treachery. I left ten mimeographed copies where they could be found by the people. If they have not been found my death would have been vain. I waited to be sure. I've come to ask."

"They were found all right," his wife cried, angrily. "And if Wolf finds you now ——"

She had scarcely spoken when an officer of the secret service suddenly laid his hand on the Bard's shoulder and quietly said:

"Come. We'll give you something to sing about now worth while!"

His wife clung to the tottering, terror-stricken figure for a moment and burst in tears. His friends shrank back in silence.

The regent had him flogged unmercifully; and Roland Adair, the Bard of Ramcat, ceased to sing. He became a mere cog in the wheel of things which moved on with swift certainty to its appointed end.

The social system worked now with deadly precision and ceaseless regularity. No citizen dared to speak against the man in authority over him or complain to the regent, for they were his trusted henchmen. Men and women huddled in groups and asked in whispers the news.

Disarmed and at the mercy of his brutal guard, cut off from the world as effectually as if they lived on another planet, despair began to sicken the strongest hearts, and suicide to be more common than in the darkest days of panic and hunger in the old world.

A curious group of three huddled together in

the shadows discussing their fate on the day the Bard was publicly flogged.

Uncle Bob led the whispered conference of woe.

"I tells ye, gemmens, dis beats de worl'! Befo' de war I wuz er slave. But I knowed my master. We wuz good friends. He say ter me, 'Bob you 'se de blackest, laziest nigger dat ebber cumber de groun'! And I laf right in his face an' say, 'Come on, Marse Henry, an' le's go fishin' — dey 'll bite ter-day'! An' he go wid me. He nebber lay de weight er his han' on me in his life. He come ter see me when I sick an' cheer me up. He gimme good clothes an' a good house an' plenty ter eat. He love me, an' I love him. I tells ye I 'se er slave now an' I don't know who de debbil my master is. Dey change him every ten days. Dey cuss an' kick me — an' I work like a beast. Dis yer comrade business too much fer me."

"To tell you the truth, boys," said a bowed figure by old Bob's side, "I lived in a model community once before."

"Oh, go 'long dar, man, dey nebber wuz er nudder one!" Bob protested.

"Yes. We all wore the same thickness of clothes, ate the same three meals regularly, never over-ate or suffered from dyspepsia; all of us worked the same number of hours a day, went to bed at the same time and got up at the same time. There was no drinking, cursing, carousing, gambling, stealing, or fighting. We were model people and every man's wants were met with absolute equality. The only trouble was we all lived in the penitentiary at San Quentin ——"

"Des listen at dat now!" Bob exclaimed.

"Yes, and I found the world outside a pretty tough place to live in when I got out, too. I thought I'd find the real thing here and slipped in. What's the difference? In the pen we wore a gray suit. We've got it here with a red spangle on it. There they decided the kind of grub they'd give us. The same here. There we worked at jobs they give us. The same here. There we worked under overseers and guards. So we do here. I was sent up there for two years. It looks like we're in here for life."

"How long, O Lord, how long, will Thy servant wait for deliverance?" cried Methodist John, in plaintive despair. "If I only could get back to the poorhouse! There I had food and shelter and clothes. It's all I've got here — but with it work, work, work! and a wicked, sinful, cussin' son of the devil always over me drivin' and watchin'!"

John's jaw suddenly dropped as a black cloud swept in from the sea and obscured the sun. A squall of unusual violence burst over the island with wonderful swiftness. The darkness of twilight fell like a pall, and a sharp peal of thunder rang over the harbour.

John watched the progress of the storm with strange elation, quietly walked through the blinding, drenching rain to the barn, and drew from the forks of two trees a lightning-rod about thirty feet long which Norman had finally made for him in answer to his constant pleading. The tip of the rod was pointed with a dozen shining spikes.

John seized this rod, held it straight over his head, and began to march with firm step around the lawn. He walked with slow, measured tread past the two big colony houses to the amazement of the people who stood at the windows watching the storm. He held his lightning-rod as a soldier a musket on dress-parade, his eyes fixed straight in front. As he passed through the floral court between the two buildings he burst into an old Methodist song, his cracked voice ringing in weird and plaintive tones with the sigh and crash of the wind among the foliage of the trees and shrubbery:

"I want to be an angel,
And with the angels stand,
A crown upon my forehead,
A harp within my hand."

Over and over he sang this stanza with increasing fervour as he marched steadily on through every path around the buildings, his rain-soaked clothes clinging to his flesh and flopping dismally about his thin legs. As the storm suddenly lifted he stopped in front of the kitchen, dropped his rod, and sank with a groan to his knees taking up again his old refrain:

"How long, O Lord, how long?"

Old Bob ran out and shook him.

"Name er God, man, what de matter wid you? Is you gone clean crazy? What you doin' monkeyin' wid dat lightnin'-rod?"

John lifted his drooping head and sighed:

"You see, neighbour, I don't like to kill myself. It's against my religion. It seems like taking things out of the hands of God. But I thought the Lord, in His infinite wisdom and mercy, might be kind enough to spare me a bolt if I lifted my rod and put myself in the way. If he had only seen fit to do it, I'd be at rest now in the courts of glory!"

"Dis here's a sad worl', brudder," Bob said comfortingly. "'Pears lak ter me de Lawd doan' lib here no mo'."

Before John could reply, a guard arrested him for disorderly conduct. The regent kicked him from his office and ordered him to prison on a diet of bread and water for a week.

The slightest criticism of his reign Wolf resented with instant and crushing cruelty. His system of spies was complete and his knowledge of every man's attitude accurate and full. Wherever he appeared, he received the most cringing obeisance.

Especially did women tremble at his approach and count themselves happy if he condescended to smile.

CHAPTER XXXIV

A BROTHER TO THE BEAST

AT THE end of three months from the time he took possession of the dredge, Wolf's men had built five duplicates, and they were all at work. More than three thousand dollars' worth of gold he weighed daily and stored in secret vaults whose keys never left his grasp.

The new colony he landed in groups of two hundred at intervals of sufficient time to assign each new member to work where the least trouble could be given. The strictest search for arms and weapons of every kind was made before each person was allowed to land.

It took only about two weeks to bring the new group into perfect subjection. Spies reported every word of surprise and criticism that fell from the lips of a newcomer.

The overseer of each gang of labourers was required to complete the task assigned to him by the standard of the very best records labour had ever made, and to secure these results it was necessary to constantly lengthen the hours of each day's service. As the efficiency of labour

306

decreased the entire colony gradually gravitated to the basis of convict service. As no man received more than food, clothes, and shelter there could be no conceivable motive to induce any one to work harder than was necessary to escape the lash of the overseer. Consequently the hours of labour were increased from nine to ten.

The one ambition now of every man was to win the favour of the authorities, and become one of the regent's guard, an overseer, or find relief from the hard, brutal tasks imposed on the great majority. The road to promotion could not be found in achievement.

The power to assign and enforce work was the mightiest force ever developed in the hand of man.

Under the system of capitalism wealth was desirable because it meant power over men. But this power was always limited. Under the free play of natural law no man, even the poorest, could be commanded to work by a superior power. He could always quit if he liked. He might choose to go hungry, or apply to the charity society for help in the last resort, but he was still master of his own person. His will was supreme. He, and he alone, could say, I will, or I will not.

Here all was changed. A new force in human history had been created. Wealth beyond all the dreams of passion and avarice was in the grasp of the regent and his henchmen. He wielded the most autocratic and merciless power over men conceivable to the human imagination — a power final and resistless, from which there could be no appeal save in death itself.

The results of this power quickly began to show in the development of life around the regent and each of his trusted minions.

By the time the theatre and music hall were finished and opened, Wolf had selected more than a hundred of the prettiest girls in the colony for the two stages.

His method of selection was always the same. The girl he desired he secretly ordered to be assigned to a dirty or disgusting form of labour. He allowed her to rave in hopeless anger at her tasks until she found that all appeal was in vain and her doom sealed.

He then made it his business to call, express his surprise at the task to which she had been assigned, and smile vaguely at her eager appeal for a change.

If she proved charming to the regent she was promptly assigned to the chorus of the State theatre and given luxurious quarters in the building adjoining.

Their tasks were light and agreeable. They studied music and dancing and elocution. But, above all, they studied day and night the art of pleasing the regent, whose frown could send any of them instantly to the washtub or the scrubbing-brush.

In like manner around the personality of each guard, overseer, secret-service man, superinten-dent, and governor of departments there grew a coterie of favoured ones whose position depended solely on the whim of the man in power.

The State only could manufacture arms. The State only could bear arms. And the system of law which Socialism developed was so full, so minute in its touch on every detail of human life, and so merciless in its system of espionage, the very idea of revolution was slowly dying in the despairing hearts of the colonists.

So sure was Wolf of his victim when once he had marked her, he was merely amused rather than displeased over Barbara's defiance of his wishes.

A few days before the opening and dedication of the regent's palace, when all his preparations were complete, Wolf summoned Catherine.

"I have here," he began, "my proclamation for the complete establishment of a perfect Social State. I publish it to-morrow morning. It goes into effect immediately:

"'From to-day the State of Ventura enters upon the reign of pure Communism which is the only logical end of Socialism. All private property is hereby abolished. The claim of husband to the person of his wife as his own can no longer be tolerated. Love is free from all chains. Marriage will hereafter be celebrated by a simple declaration before a representative of the State, and it shall cease to bind at the will of either party. Complete freedom in the sex-relationship is left to the judgment and taste of a race of equally developed men and women. The State will interfere, when necessary, to regulate the birth-rate and maintain the limits of efficient population.'"

"Which means for me?" Catherine inquired.

"That you are divorced and free to marry whom you please."

The woman uttered a cry of anguish, threw her arms around Wolf's big neck, and burst into sobs.

"Oh, Herman, surely you have some pity left in your heart! For God's sake, don't cast me out of your life in this cruel, horrible way!"

He turned his stolid face away with cold indifference.

She lifted her tapering hand timidly and smoothed the coarse hair back from his forehead with a tender gesture.

"Can you forget," she went on, in low, passionate tones, "all we have been to one another through the long, dark years of our fight with poverty and oppression? All I have done for your sake?

That I broke my husband's heart—for he loved me even as I love you—I left my babies, and have never seen them since; broke with every friend and loved one on earth for you!   Have you forgotten all I have done in this work?   The tireless zeal with which I 've fought your battles? Can you kick me from your presence now as though I were a dog?"

Wolf pursed his thick lips and scowled.

"No, I mean that you shall stay where you are and take charge of my new household.   Barbara will need your assistance."

"Barbara!" she gasped.

"I have chosen her as the new regent," Wolf calmly answered.   "I will announce our marriage at the dedication of the palace."

"And you think that I will accept such shame?"

"I 'm sure you will!" he quickly answered with an ominous threat in his tone.

The woman sprang to her feet and faced him, her tall, lithe figure tense with passion.

"I dare you to try it!"

"Dare?" Wolf repeated in a low growl.

"I said it!" she cried, defiantly.   "From the very housetop I 'll shout the story of our life.   I 'll show you   I 'm a power you must reckon with ——"

"And I 'll show you, " Wolf answered "that

there's but one power that counts now in the world of realities in which we live — the elemental force of tooth, and nail, and claw — do you understand?"

He thrust his big, ugly face into hers and a look of terror flashed from her eyes as she saw his features convulsed with fury.

"Please, Herman!" she pleaded at last in a feeble, childish voice.

"You are still daring me?"

"No, I give up — surely you will not strike me!" she gasped.

"Not unless I have to," he answered, with cold menace.

CHAPTER XXXV

LOVE AND LOCKSMITHS

BARBARA sat in the little rose bower on the lawn puzzling her brain for the thousandth time over impossible schemes to communicate with Norman.

From day to day she had watched with increasing fear the rapid growth of Wolf's cruel instincts under the conditions of tyranny he had established.

She had appealed in vain to every man in authority. Everywhere the same answer. The regent's power inspired a terror which no appeal could penetrate.

She started with a sudden thought. Among the guards who stood watch at Wolf's door was the nineteen-year-old boy who had acted as usher and shown Norman to a seat in the Socialist Hall the night they met.

She had caught a peculiar look in his face the last time she entered Wolf's office. Could it be possible he was in love with her in the helpless, heroic, boy fashion of his age? She would put him to the test. It was worth trying.

She found him on guard in the corridor outside

Wolf's door, approached him cautiously, touched his hand timidly, and whispered:

"Jimmy, I 'm in great distress."

"I wish I could help you, Miss Barbara," he answered in low, earnest tones, sweeping the corridor with a quick look.

"Even at the risk of your life?"

"I 'd jump at the chance to die for you!" was the simple answer.

Barbara's voice choked and her little hand caught the boy's gratefully. His conquest was too easy, his love too big and generous! "I wish I could do it, Jimmy, without letting you risk your life, but I must see Norman."

"I 'll help you if I can, Miss Barbara, but I don't know how. The jailer won't let me in without an order from the regent."

"I 'll go in now," she went on, "get a piece of paper from his desk, forge the order, and sign his name. I can imitate his handwriting. I 'll give it to you immediately, and watch until you get back to your post."

"I 'll do it!" the boy answered, his eyes shining.

"Tell Norman," Barbara whispered, "that I have found Saka in the hills. He has built a skiff and has it ready to sail with his message for relief."

"I understand."

She entered Wolf's office unannounced and surprised him with her girlish buoyancy of spirit.

With a light laugh she sprang on his big desk, sat down among his papers, and deftly closed her hand over one of his small official order-pads.

"I cannot see Norman, to-day?" she asked.

"Not to-day, my dear. A little later, yes, but not to-day!"

He laughed carelessly and turned in his arm-chair to a messenger:

"Take that order to the captain of the guard and tell him to report to me at seven o'clock to-night."

While he spoke, the girl slipped from her place on the desk and thrust the order pad in her pocket.

"Then I 'm wasting breath to plead with you?"

"Decidedly. But I congratulate you on the rational way you are beginning to look at things."

As she moved to the door she smiled over her shoulder: "Time will work wonders, perhaps!"

"I told you so," he laughed.

She hurried to her room and wrote the order signing Wolf's name without a moment's hesitation:

"Admit the guard bearing this order for the delivery of a personal message to the prisoner, Norman Worth.

"WOLF — *Regent*."

She stood at the window and watched the boy enter the jail. He stayed an interminable time! Each tick of the tiny watch in her hand seemed an hour. One minute, two, three, four, five minutes slowly dragged. Merciful God, would he never return? A thousand questions began to strangle her. Had Wolf suspected and played with her? Had the jailer recognized the trick and arrested the boy? Had Wolf discovered the boy's absence from his post?

She looked at her watch again. He had been gone seven minutes! The door of the jail suddenly opened and the boy appeared.

Her hand was tingling with a curious pain. She looked, and the nails of her fingers had cut the flesh as she had stood in agony counting the seconds.

The boy walked with leisurely precision as though on an ordinary errand for the regent. Barbara waited until he resumed his position on guard at the door and quickly reached his side.

He pressed a note into her hand, whispering:

"The jailer held me up at first — but I found him!"

Barbara glanced down the corridor with a quick look threw her arms around the boy's neck and kissed him tenderly.

He smiled, drew a deep breath, and said:

"Now, I'm ready to die!"

"No. To live and fight," she cried. "Fight our way back to freedom. You must help me!"

She turned and flew to her room. The note in her hand was burning the soft flesh.

She locked her door and read:

"Heart of My Heart:

"Iron bars have held my body but my soul has been with you! I've seen you walking among the flowers a hundred times and tried to force my message through the walls. I enclose a telegram to my father and one to the Governor of California. Send Saka to Santa Barbara with them. The troops should arrive in forty-eight hours. All I ask of God now is the chance to fight. I love you!

"Always yours,
NORMAN."

She kissed the note, tore it into fragments, and burned the pieces.

When night had fallen, Jimmy safely passed the patrol lines, delivered his message to Saka, helped him launch the skiff, watched the little sail spread before a fair wind, and returned to his post.

CHAPTER XXXVI

THE SHINING EMBLEM

WHEN Wolf's patrol telephoned two days later that a company of troops had suddenly landed on the other side of the island, he called the captain of the guard:

"A detail of men to move the gold aboard the ship. Order the steam up. I'll divide with you. We must beat those soldiers back until we can sail. Fight them at every possible stand as they cross the hills. I'll join you if the guard is driven in."

The captain hurried to execute Wolf's orders, while the regent began with feverish haste to transfer the treasures of the colony to the ship.

Norman sat on his cot in prison, awaiting anxiously the first sound of the troops.

He suddenly leaped to his feet.

"They are coming!"

Listening a moment intently, he cried:

"There it is again — the scream of fifes from the hills! — now, they are driving in the pickets —

hear the crack of those rifles! — God in heaven, is n't it music!"

He sank back on the cot with a sob of joy.

In a rush the troops surrounded the jail. The sheriff lifted his hand and shouted:

"In the name of the peace and dignity of the State of California ——"

Wolf answered with a defiant wave and charged at the head of his guard. The soldiers poured into their ranks a deadly fire. At the first volley the leader fell. The charging column hesitated, halted, threw down their arms, and surrendered.

In five minutes Colonel Worth entered the jail and father and son silently embraced. Barbara followed and Norman clasped her in his arms.

A shout rose from the troops and the group within moved to the prison window. The colour-sergeant had hauled down the red ensign of Socialism from the flag-staff on the lawn and lifted the Stars and Stripes in its place.

Norman's hand sought his father's. They clasped a moment tremblingly, and, still looking through the barred window at the shining emblem in the sky, the young man slowly said:

"It *is* beautiful, is n't it Governor!"

THE END